Homesick for Earth

# HOMESICK for EARTH

Olivia Schanzer

Matchlock Press
New York

*Homesick for Earth*
by Olivia Schanzer



Sobeki language adapted from
*Field Book of Wild Birds & Their Music,*
by F. Schuyler Mathews
(New York: Putnam's Sons, 1921,
reprint, Mineola: Dover Publications, 1967)

Library of Congress Control Number: 2016902096
ISBN: 978-1-939333-04-9

Version 1.0

Published by Matchlock Press
PO Box 90606
Brooklyn, NY 11209
matchlock.com

*For my dear daughter,*
*Valis, and for all the other*
*future coral gardeners.*

# Homesick for Earth

ЗЕМЛЯ

# I

In front of you is a picture of a little girl named Vera Yevgenyevna Mironova. That is her name when she is on Earth, anyway. Her mother and father have taught her that it is always more polite to introduce yourself in your host's language. If your host is trying to be polite to you as well, you may find that you have a problem, with each person talking only in the other's language! This is especially bad if neither one of you speaks the other's language very well.

As Vera's parents have told her repeatedly, it does not do to be too particular about what you eat or what you are called when traveling beyond Earth. On Sobek, Vera's name is

It sounds nothing at all like our name "Vera," but it has something in common with it, being a similar sort of name, and occurring with similar frequency in the population. It is a pretty and somewhat old-fashioned name, popular in many languages on their world, and connotes in the minds of the populace a small bouquet of violets, soft furry leaves included, in an old glass vase on a breakfast table.

The people of Sobek have a hard time saying many of our consonants. Their spoken language is made up of hissing, clucking and whistling sounds passed down from their more horizontal ancestors, who looked—let us be frank—a bit like the Komodo dragons of Earth, but with whiskers. The inhabitants of that planet have very different tongues than we do, but while they have trouble pronouncing most Earth languages, they can make many noises at birth that linguists from our planet must work their whole lives to master.

Though they are too polite to laugh, they find the way we talk to be extremely amusing. They would not say so—except in the most delicate and discreet hand gestures—but they are amazed by our tongues and consider them, with a certain degree of condescension, to be blunt instruments, slabs of meat not at all up to the task of communication. The first Sobeki visitors to Earth sent back dispatch after dispatch on this one topic, all published in their newspapers, as the public never seemed to tire of it.

Just try to order a cup of Earth coffee there! You might find yourself repeating your order several times as a crowd forms around you, leaning in to hear your vocalizations. It is even possible that some of them will try to peer into your mouth and get a look at your tongue. If you can stand to do so, it's always nice to be sociable and show it to them, though I wouldn't let them reach into your mouth to feel it, for at that point in your travels you may not have built up a good immunity to their local germs.

Although you have seen a picture of Vera, I'm sure you know—unless you have been very badly brought up—that the way you look is not the whole of you, but only a small part. Unless you are very wicked, you would not ascribe good manners and kindness to someone just because you thought their hair was pretty. But sometimes your body does influence how you are around other people, and Vera is very tall for her age, which contributes to her bossiness. She would be the first to tell you that she was, though she won't like it if you point it out yourself, as is the case with most people and their faults, no matter how frank they are in mentioning them.

At home in Moscow, she liked to tell you that she was the second-tallest person in Ms Utkina's class, and each summer during break, she drank enormous quantities of milk and spent a great deal of her time atop the jungle gym, where the sunshine was strongest, in order to overtake the lead. Yet despite all her efforts, the fall always saw that position in the hands of a boy named Dmitri with whom no one got along. It seemed that he spent the summer working on his height as well.

It was all the worse since Dmitri was so unpleasant. No one likes to see advantages in the hands of people one finds distasteful, and worse still was the way he used his height to bad ends, shouldering people aside and knocking them to the ground whenever he could get away with it. In the name of justice and as an agent of cosmic retribution, Vera planned to knock him down herself the minute she had an inch on him, and she spoke frequently about her plans at lunch over the cafeteria's hot borscht, which she liked very much.

"When he's down I might press my foot on him," she confided to her friends, "but only for a moment or two."

As the second-tallest person in the class, she had come close in pursuit of this goal, but had never knocked him so that he stayed down. Certainly he had never been down long enough for her to apply her sneaker to his anatomy. Here I must caution you not to report any part of this to Vera's mother. Though she was perfectly well-equipped for her own self-defense, as a member of the United Planets Diplomatic Corps she advocated de-escalation at all times.

*Dmitri eating glue, and who knows what he will wash it down with!*

"You may not like his behavior, Verochka, but unsolicited shoving is an offensive, not a defensive, act," her mother said. "You may return a shove fairly, but you may not shove him out of the blue. Besides, your premeditation is a mile thick. You've been going on about it to anyone who would listen since the moment he appeared."

"You can't punch that big baby," her father added, looking up from the advice column in the most recent issue of *Galactic Translator*. "You'll be stuck with the punishment when the teacher sees him crying." It was true that when Dmitri wasn't knocking people over, he whined a great deal and couldn't stand the taste of any sauce he'd already ladled out over the goose. I'm sure there's something sad at the bottom of all this, but this is not Dmitri's story, thank goodness! Otherwise we would be forced to spend more than one chapter discussing the eating of glue, which he did as a matter of teatime most afternoons!

For her part, Vera's story has been an ordinary one, much like yours or mine. I do not spend the majority of my time watching the behavior of chimpanzees from under a blind, or have a job filling hot-air balloons just before dawn (which is when they are always filled), and unless you are very lucky, I suspect you are not being taught your multiplication tables by the clowns at the circus where your acrobatic parents are employed (and with whom you travel here and there around the world by caravan and train). If your mother is a sea captain and your father tastes the king's lunch for poison, then perhaps you might stop reading immediately (for what do you need with books?) and go and stand at the prow of the ship and watch the waves for porpoises, or assist your father with the stewed prunes (but gingerly!) if he is cavalier enough to let you. But Vera, until recently, did not live a life like that. For the most part, she had the joys and boredoms of a regular childhood. Some days are trips to the beach. Some are the dull, endless cleaning of closets. There are boxes of chocolate. There is cold leftover chicken for the third day in a row.

A great deal of the time, Vera, like children everywhere, was engaged in amusing herself not with the grand or important, but with those activities that could take place in a very nice though scuffed-up apartment in Moscow, where the radiators were loud but kept the house warm in the winter, and the cupboards in the kitchen were full of food; which is to say, it was a home pleasant and dull, the aspiration of most adults.

She collected coins, pressed flowers between the pages of her books, and had a series of small dolls that lived on a shelf of their own, and with which she sometimes played simply by staring at them, for they engaged in strange rivalries and intrigues even when she was not arranging them. She was ensconced in this apartment, having lived there all her life, and she was comfortable there.

The rest of her life was much the same. Vera had a large extended family, and she was surrounded by open-hearted neighbors and beloved friends she had known since kindergarten, and she attended, much to the happiness of herself and her parents, a Strugatsky school—a place of great intellectual rigor and fellowship.

Though she liked most of the children, she had two best friends in her pod at school, Olia and Dasha, with whom she fought all the time, for all three girls were extremely strong-willed. Nevertheless, they were very close and enjoyed each

*A sample of Vera's collections: a little doll from Holland, and an array of coins, including, at lower right, the jewel of her collection, the precious Spintzner five-cent piece, a coin misprinted with two instead of one antennæ on the head of Octavio Spintzner.*

other's company. Perhaps, though they wouldn't say it, they even enjoyed the fights and disagreements. Who can account for another person's tastes? The three girls had formed a private club by means of stationery; they drew the logo on top of each page, a little dirty swan to whom they fed peanuts in Gorky Park. He had been christened Snezhok, which was the name of the club.

Together they liked to listen to the radio and assemble notebooks, one of which involved clipping and pasting photographs of comely horses from their grandfathers' racing forms. On her own, Vera also kept a botanical notebook with sketches and detailed descriptions, as her aunt was a botanist and frequently took her to the gardens.

All of this has been a very fair and accurate catalogue of Vera's life on Earth. She was sociable, a little headstrong, with widely varied interests and a desire and enthusiasm for new experiences. She was a good friend and a formidable adversary, and had an aura of bravery and good humor about her. But an uprooted Vera hardly conformed to this description. Besides her same long ponytail, same cheeks and chin, Vera was unrecognizable.

For years she had longed for adventure and thought she had all the tools to meet it. Her grandmother had started her on a subscription to the Explorers Club newsletter; though it was written for adults, she read it avidly. She frequently imagined better parents for herself (spangled and hanging from the trapeze), wondered why she was stuck on dry land, and like so many of us, brooded over the fact that, though deserving, she had never met a monkey face-to-face when movie stars always seemed to have one near.

Now that adventure was actually before her, Vera hid in-

*From left: Olia, Vera and Dasha. Olia is a short girl who is sometimes a bit bossy, and Dasha is a tall girl who has been spoiled quite a bit, and so also gets bossy, and Vera, of course, come to think of it, is bossy as well.*

side, and even looked out the window timidly with the drape held close, so that she could draw it around her if someone looked up from the street. There were new plants and animals all around outside, but she hadn't added anything to her notebook. Her collections as well sat dormant in their boxes. She had not even opened them to see if they had survived the trip. She was too afraid to check; they were her last link to Earth, after all.

This was all because Vera was now two thousand light-years away from home, which meant she would have to cross two star clusters and the Ghost of Jupiter if she so much as wanted to eat a cherry pirozhok.

# II

At home in Moscow, Vera had felt only excitement at the prospect of the trip. Her parents, however, could not conceal their anxiety from her.

They sat gravely at the dining room table, stew untouched. "My dear," said Vera's mother, "we are considering a move." Staring her down, they clutched their drinking glasses. Her father exhibited a slight twitch at the corner of his mouth. Fearful expectations could be heard in their tight, tremulous voices, but Vera responded cheerfully. "I'd love it!" she said. Her zeal did not dissipate even after they explained where they intended to go. "Best idea you've ever had!"

They tried to quell her enthusiasm.

"You know, you might find yourself very sad at times," said her mother, with the intense and probing eye contact of a therapist-trainee at the Moscow Clinic.

"And angry at us," said her father, reaching to hold her hand across the table and squeezing it intermittently. It occurred to Vera that there must be a new manual on breaking bad news somewhere in the apartment.

"And lonely," added her mother, and paused, unsure of what further support to give.

But Vera disagreed vehemently. "I can't wait to get there! I'm going to record everything that happens and send home the news."

"That's a very good idea, dear," said her mother, who was obviously thrown by Vera's reaction. "You might find it helps you to sort out your feelings."

Each night at dinner, Vera's parents tried to engage her on the topic, but Vera did not see their point of view.

"Why would I be upset?" she asked repeatedly.

"It's natural to be upset. Moving has always made me uneasy," said her father. "Your mother and I don't like to be parted from our Turkish coffee."

"Can't you bring it with you?"

"Only if you smuggle in the beans. Foodstuffs rarely survive quarantine." Vera did not find her father's tone at all convincing. She knew her parents to be deep-dyed adventurers. It was obvious from their family history.

The plan was to leave at the end of the school year. Before then, there was packing and sorting, and parties at school and at home. They were much busier than they had ever been. They bought shade hats and sand goggles, and Vera and her mother went from drug store to drug store filling the *United Planets List of Necessary Items for Earth People on Sobek*. It was a packing list for a strange sort of sleepaway camp; instead of rain pants and water sandals, it listed chemical compounds, powders, tinctures and basic elements. Many things were not available on Sobek, and Earth people were expected to bring the Sobeki doctors all the ingredients that they might need for medicines. Whether or not they would know how to use them effectively after paging through the out-of-date editions of Earth medical textbooks that the UP Panel on Intersolar Friendship had sent them was something about which explorers chose not to think.

Vera heard her parents muttering about it one evening. "I only wish I'd taken that field medicine course when it was offered to me," her father said.

"Please don't worry, Yevgeny," replied her mother. "I'll

*A selection from the* United Planets List of Necessary Items for Earth People on Sobek. *The poisonous pills at the front are for rubbing on particularly bad foot fungus.*

practice a tourniquet on you later this evening. The most important thing is to stop you from bleeding out." Still, Vera was not at all nervous.

As for clothing, if they needed something new the tailors there could make it, but it would be much more expensive than just buying off-the-rack on Earth, for Sobeki dimensions were not too close to the dimensions of human beings. Furthermore, there were not many tailors beyond those that made theatrical costumes, since the Sobekis did not usually wear clothes.

The shopping went quickly to tedium even if one liked to shop, as each member of the family needed to be shod (there was no chance of finding shoes on Sobek!), behatted, and girded with several years' worth of underwear.

"Be thankful we aren't going to Achernar 5. It's so cold at Moon Base Kalpana Chawla, you'll lose your nose if you don't keep it covered!" said her mother as they looked through the suntan lotions at the pharmacy.

The parties were constant, for news of their departure had spread throughout the neighborhood. Besides the expected friends and neighbors, they were feted by the mongers at the fish store on the corner, who boiled up a gigantic soup in the middle of the street. When they went in to buy stamps, the mail carriers at the post office brought out cherry juice in plastic cups and a secret bottle of vodka to toast them, and they carried on with the party for the rest of the afternoon after the Mironovs had left.

There was great excitement surrounding their trip, for it was still not so common for a family from their neighborhood to move to another planet. Maybe it was somewhat of a provincial neighborhood (it's possible), but whatever the reason, their acquaintances foisted sweets and cordials on them wherever they went. You can't fault people for their enthusiasm and interest, however, and the Mironovs certainly did not want to leave behind snubs. As a result, Vera's parents remained slightly tipsy for two straight weeks.

The Strugatsky School planned their own party for Vera, and all the children from the other classrooms were invited. "A very fine thing," said the headmaster, "to have an ambassador among our ranks. We must praise Vera's bravery and pluck!" Even the ladies and gentlemen who filed forms in the office came, though they were very busy at this time of year, and were usually unwilling to put down their work.

Ms Lapidus, who answered the phones, crocheted Vera a palm-sized globe of the Earth with an arrow pointing to home. "But don't forget us, my little dear," said the woman. "I will look for your star every evening, though I don't suppose I'll find it."

Vera was extremely touched, for she saw that Ms Lapidus had shed a tear. She gave her a hug, and after that, Vera remembered to stop by and chat with her every day until the school year ended.

The gym was being fumigated, so the party had to be held in the auditorium, the only other room large enough to accommodate all the students. This was an awkward place for a party, and the sight of the dais with its unclaimed microphone infected the adults with the need to declaim, so that almost every teacher, and quite a number of students, got up to give speeches.

There was a sheet cake with the heft of a small pony, carried in on a litter by a crew of sturdy bakers. The speeches went on so long that the decision was made to break with tra-

*Some little boys and a girl from Vera's school lead the auditorium in an inappropriate song in Vera's honor. What the inappropriate song was I cannot tell you. It was very rude and made the teachers blush, though they were unable to cut it off before the children were done.*

dition and serve the cake before they were done, even though it was extremely impolite to have the children filing by while people were still talking. Each class lined up in turn, and there were high spirits and some splashing of fruit punch.

"To our great friend Vera," said Olia and Dasha in unison at the microphone, holding aloft their plastic cups (they were left over from the previous winter's holiday party, and had a ruddy-faced Father Christmas on the side), "bravest cosmonaut and Earth ambassador!"

The principal presented Vera with a little engraved medal from the school. It was true he had a small budget for medals, and although it was the sort of job that he usually delegated, he was fond of ordering them himself. On the back it read: "Ms Utkina's class, The Strugatsky School, sends Vera love and greetings from Earth." The principal pinned it to Vera's sweater. It drooped sadly, and Vera, who like any reasonable child had always wanted her own medal with an incidental engraving, vowed to get an appropriate setting for it in the form of a jacket, navy style.

The principal was an extremely sentimental gentleman, possibly a little fond of morning schnapps in his coffee cup, and he shed a tear on either side of his big red nose as he delivered a long and rambling speech about the first time he went to sleepaway camp. "The long, dark nights may drag out—nights filled with the strange sounds of animals that you cannot name. At least you, my dear, will have your Mama and Papa nearby. You will not be alone with only pimple-faced schoolboys to comfort you—inadequately—when you cry."

The crowd fidgeted and swayed politely, for the children at the Strugatsky School were very tactful, and had learned

*The very medal that Vera received ceremoniously in the auditorium of the Strugatsky School. The gentlemen depicted on the medal are the Strugatsky brothers, and about them I'm sure you already know a great deal.*

not to shout “Get down from there!” impatiently, or throw spitballs. They had had a special assembly about the hygienic problems of spitballs, in fact.

Vera was delighted by the whole affair. How rare it is for one child to be the guest of honor at such an event. She hadn’t done anything at all to earn it! Her classmates pounded her on the back, gently cuffed her ears, and hugged her tightly. How much they seemed to care for her and she for them.

As the party wore on, Vera started to feel uncomfortable. A cosmonaut, she thought to herself, should be more resistant to sentimentality. “Actually, I’m tired of Moscow,” she told one little boy haughtily. “I’ve been here a very long time already.”

The little boy was much impressed by her nonchalance. Once, at an autograph signing, he had met a real cosmonaut and had seen this same attitude. He had a sudden impulse to ask Vera for her autograph on the cover of his notebook. She obliged him gladly, and added a small drawing of a rocket ship next to her name, which, unbeknownst to Vera, was exactly the same way the cosmonaut had signed her own name.

## III

VERA walked by the Moscow Explorers Club on ulitsa Ilinka frequently on the way to swim classes with her babysitter. The club frequently played host to explorers returning from space, who would stand at the podium with the big map of the galaxy behind them and recount their adventures. Vera had always imagined herself delivering just such an address. Once, when her parents were scheduled to deliver a talk there, Vera fell ill and had to stay at home with her grandmother. It was an extremely disappointing turn of events, and she had never gotten to go back and see the great hall, that map, or the famous mural of the founding of the United Planets.

Vera saw herself as an explorer, simply one who hadn't yet done the exploring. She had been raised by UP translators, after all, and she viewed their stories and packing skills as her heredity.

Regarding the translators in question, they were preparing diligently, as her parents always did when getting ready to enter a new culture. In the evenings, the family sat together on the couch and listened to recordings of the odd music of the planet. Sobeki music was really quite incomprehensible to human ears. Some of it was from a hissing and percussive form of folk song that was done in the round, some like simple mumbling, and some almost beyond Vera's ability to hear.

"Please don't put the folk music on while we're eating," her mother said to her father when he seemed to be making his way to the stereo. "It gives me globus."

The music wasn't the kind of thing an Earth child could pick up very quickly and sing along to, unless you are the sort of child who is good enough at imitating bird calls that birds will respond to them. Still, they managed to sing along to a few of them, in the way that you might join in with a visiting *chickadee-dee-dee-dee-dee-dee.*

While they listened, they sat in a line on the couch and read magazines together, paging through them and handing them off until they were quite ragged. They all liked the animal fashion magazines the best. The Sobekis generally did not prefer to wear clothes, although they liked to accessorize, but they dressed their riding animals extravagantly. Those handsome beasts could be seen in any number of hats, capelets and goggles, fanciful headdresses and foot coverings. They seemed not to mind, and they always looked quite cheerful in the photographs.

There was also a box of water-stained Sobeki children's magazines that the former ambassador had left behind when she and her family decamped. Vera's parents read her the folktales they contained with great animation, and labored together over the word puzzles, which—though intended for ten-year-old Sobeki children—contained many challenging colloquialisms. It was true that everything about these children seemed strange. They had strange hobbies and played strange games, kept strange pets and ate strange foods. But Vera would not have uttered these words aloud; it was very poor form. Strange, her parents had cautioned her, was not a way to refer to the doings of others.

"What if they are cannibals?" Vera asked.

"Then the proper term," her mother said, "is 'horrific.'

*A selection of magazines from Sobek. Note especially, at the back, a magazine consisting entirely of man-on-the-street photos of footslogs in their many and varied fashions. They are a vain species, and take particular delight in their capes and headgear.*

You can't mince words about that."

Vera pored over the material, listening diligently to her language tapes whenever she had a moment, and greatly outpacing the hour a day that her parents had prescribed.

Each evening over cocoa, she practiced sightreading from the phrasebook with her mother. Vera might say:

which meant: "May I have a swazzlefruit, and a straw with which to drink it, please?" To which her mother would reply:

This meant: "Would you like to stay and sip it here while you tell me the local gossip?" That was the conventional response, for as her father told her, "They have a long, storied tradition of gossip, and don't look down on it as we do. It is considered a respectable way to pass the time, in fact, like solving chess puzzles."

It was only when she met for the last time with her two best friends, Olia and Dasha, at their secret spot behind the post office that she was struck with the idea that it might be sad to say goodbye to her friends or to Earth.

"I want to give you something," said Olia, and took from

her schoolbag her lavender sticker album. Vera gasped. The sticker album, puffy as a turnover, somewhat dingier in color than at purchase, had been owned first by Olia's oldest sister, then by her middle sister, and then by Olia. It was as close to an heirloom as children—who are not very old after all—can create among themselves.

Once, Olia left it on the bus, and ran after it for many blocks, shouting at the driver all the while: "Stop! Stop! An emergency of life and death!" The driver—when he finally caught sight of the crazed, sweaty Olia flagging him down in his rear-view mirror—turned bone-white, and stopped the bus so short that several people fell over. Then he ran out and shook her, shrieking, "What is it?! Oh Lord, tell me I haven't run a man over again!" Needless to say, the whole bus proceeded to shout when they heard what the cause was. She was defended by no one, poor Olia, as no one saw the import of her stickers. It didn't help matters that the exhausted driver left the passengers where they were to go on his break, so rattled were his nerves. At that point, Olia ran away quickly with her album, hoping no one from the bus would recognize her and tell her parents.

"No, no. I can't take the album," Vera said. "Just give me a sticker or two, or you'll have nothing left to trade." Vera didn't want to take it. She said no several times, but Olia pressed it on her.

"It's better for me: I'll start over from scratch. And what if they don't have stickers on Sobek? After all, one needs the comforts of home."

"I'll return it to you when I come back," Vera said, "in a year or two."

"Will you be back then?" Dasha asked cautiously.

*What does this sticker album contain? If you are a collector, you know that it is not so much what it contains but the manner in which the contents are organized. Olia's eldest sister, who began the collection and passed it down, formulated a complicated system that took into consideration no less than ten rubrics by which a sticker should be judged. The connoisseur finds that the inside of this album is unimpeachable, æsthetically. Tucked into a pocket at the back is a list of criteria, so that those who add to the collection can be in compliance.*

For the first time, Vera considered when she would return. Perhaps her parents intended to keep her in space forever. She would have to ask them. They had not mentioned a return trip, after all; it was true that there was a permanence to their plans. Even still, their apartment would stay where it was: full of their furniture, though with a strange family among it—the Kovalevskys, two doctors and a wombat.

Dasha too presented Vera with a cherished object, a coral bracelet that had been in her family for many generations. She pulled it from a velvet pouch within a cardboard box that she had padded down with newspaper, and she would not even let Vera unwrap it, but unwrapped it herself.

It had been a very long time since coral had been strung for bracelets, and a great many scientists had worked for centuries repairing the reefs, measuring them and re-seeding them. They even had a group at the UP, under the ægis of the well-regarded International Ocean Salinity Council, called "The Coral Gardeners Group," which coordinated efforts in that direction. Before Vera was born, her parents had worked for a year at the Salinity Council, which was located in The Hague, in the building that used to house the International Criminal Court.

"No, no," said Vera. "Your mother will be angry with you. This is just too valuable. Besides, you know that it's contraband. It can't be moved from place to place; they won't even let it in the spaceport."

"She's right," Olia agreed.

"I suppose so," said Dasha, who, quite frankly, was relieved that she didn't have to part with her bracelet. "Look, I'll give you my t-shirt, but you can't lose it, okay?" It was a funny thing, but the elderly t-shirt was worth almost as much to her as the priceless bracelet. Dasha wore the t-shirt, decorated with spooning kittens, almost every day. It was so threadbare that her mother, who did spoil her a little, had to hand-wash it. "And here, this too," said Dasha, removing a small daisy barrette, and catching several hairs as she extracted it. Later, Vera put the barrette in her jewelry box for safekeeping, long red curly hair and all.

Vera had not forgotten to bring gifts for her friends, either. She wanted them to remain close across the light-years, as close as they were now when they could see each other every day. They would no longer be able to sip their kompot in the lunchroom together or walk home hand in hand, but they would be reminded of one another when they looked in the mirror each morning. So she strung bead necklaces for all three of them, and from each dangled a tin locket upon which Vera had written in red nail polish borrowed from her mother, "O-D-V." That was all she could fit on the back, no love, no greetings. In the available space, "O-D-V" would have to suffice. She did not have time, in and among her preparations, to get a smaller brush.

It was a solemn moment for the three of them, and they consecrated it with a ritual, which was what they always did at their most serious moments. When you want to seal something, it is best to do it formally. Even adults know this, for handshakes, signatures, the exchange of presents, the sharing of drinks and food, all these rituals come directly from the child's knowledge that we must seal our words.

First they wrote on paper, in the clearest and most legal phrases they could muster, a promise to be lifelong friends. Olia's mother was a lawyer, and she had once given them a template for binding contracts, which from frequent use

*Vera, Olia and Dasha consecrate their friendship in flame.*

they had quickly committed to memory. Then they signed the document, and pulled hairs from their heads. Of course, you must pull hairs from heads for binding contracts; that is the responsibility of paralegals at the better law firms.

They made a little stone circle out of gravel, and burned it all up, promises and hair, with matches that Vera had taken from her father; he did not keep track of his matches at all. Then they waited until the little fire went out—it really wasn't much, if you are concerned—and each of them took a pinch of the ashes and put it in her locket. At that moment, Vera felt her goodbyes weighing heavily around her neck, and she found that she was crying a little, too.

Then they hugged. They stamped on the place where their little fire had been, though it was certainly out already. They spat a little on it as well. They were very responsible girls, even if they occasionally set fires behind the post office. A mail carrier at the end of his rounds appeared, pulling his cart behind him, and caught sight of what they were doing.

"Is that ashes? My goodness, I don't smell smoke, do I? What criminal class is this? Tiny little criminals? Are you street urchins? Little pickpockets?"

Then he noticed who the girls were. He delivered mail to all three and knew their families. His name was Mr Bobrik, and he wore a handsome chess player's beard to keep his neck warm in the winter. This past December—for the solstice—Vera's parents had given him a platter of dried fruit and a bottle of vodka, the very bottle that had been used to toast the family at the post office party the previous week. He had not been present for the toasting, though, and had been disheartened to find his bottle empty come Monday morning. When it was explained to him why it had been drained,

*The postman is beside himself at the thought of Vera and her family among ravening iguanadons. He gives as well a grisly description of the imagined scene, which only succeeds in scaring him worse, though the children are unaffected.*

however, he forgave them immediately for drinking it.

"Vera!" he exclaimed. "You are the girl who is going to live among the lizards. My word, you must be terrified! I shiver for you, you poor dear. I told my wife it's child abuse. The Children's Council must have your parents arrested for this crime. They must stop you before you get on the ship, in the name of all sense and reason. Whatever will you do among the lizards? Who will play with you? My goodness, they'll have you subsisting on boiled flies!"

The girls laughed at that, and the mailman furrowed his brow. "You laugh now, but perhaps they don't even eat flies; flies are very small for creatures of that size. They'd have to be eating all day to get any nourishment. Who's to say that this poor girl won't be eaten herself! I don't suppose you'll laugh when they mail her bones back to Moscow for burial!"

"What a horrible thing to say," said Dasha, and then they all laughed again, a little nervously this time.

"I am sorry for that. My wife always has to remind me not to scare children. Anyway, I suppose it's probably unlikely that you'll be eaten," he said, and he gave them all toffees from his pocket before going inside sheepishly.

It wasn't until much later, when she was already in deep space, that Vera remembered the mailman's expression of terror, his talk of flies, and the way he forgot immediately to be mad about the fire—although setting public fires no matter how small was a serious offense—and she realized that just possibly what he said was not funny at all. Vera was heading to a planet entirely populated not by men or women as we know them, but by massive upright lizards. Who was to say that these creatures—with their strong jaws and immense hands, beclawed and wrapped in the armor of their thick reptilian skin—would not develop a taste for human meat and divvy up the delicacies before them: her father, her mother and Vera herself? Not enough for dinner, but perhaps for canapés?

## IV

So you are faced with a vision of our protagonist, her limbs halfway down the spectacular green maw of a several-storeys-high iguanadon. Perhaps you too are wondering, like the agitated mail carrier, over Mr and Mrs Mironov's judgment. A number of possibilities have probably even presented themselves by now as to the sort of people her parents are, none that paint them in a very good light.

What sort of people relocate their precious daughter to a dangerous planet full of scaly brutes? Perhaps they are even the type of parents who simply act on their own whims no matter how slight or transient, without regard to their child's well-being. Perhaps they are people too restless to stay in one place for very long, and in another lifetime might have been tinkers, traveling from town to town in a wagon, tools jangling and so forth. People like that are glad to sleep at day's end on a bed of hay, finding mattresses, after many years on the road, too smooth and soft.

None of these things! In fact, Mr and Mrs Mironov are extremely sober people with extremely serious jobs. As the chairman of the UP put it in his speech at the UP Congress Winter Party last year: "They," and here he did not simply mean Vera's father and mother but all those in the diplomatic corps, "are the glue between the worlds, the reason we are able to share resources with the sharp-minded people of Quattuor Tempora, or have gotten the advice of the Slompernauts about how best to repair our coral reefs." (It is the Slompernauts who are the original Coral Gardeners, and introduced us to their many-tomed encyclopedia, the *Coralliorum Pandectes*, without which I shudder to think where our oceans would be now.)

Vera's parents were not actually responsible for the business with the Slompernauts, nor were they themselves the ones who made contact with "the sharp-minded people of Quattuor Tempora," but they have done much good work in their own right as translators for the United Planets. They are objectively fine translators, and between them they speak any number of Earth languages; perhaps they have even lost count. They speak as well two varieties of Adharan and the base language of the Canopus solar system from which all the Sonorian dialects come.

They were both gifted linguists from an early age, with proficient and well-tuned ears, but now sometimes they sat down at eight in the morning over oatmeal with a local newspaper before them, and by dinner were chatting cheerfully with strangers about the care of their cats' ear mites, which is to say, using the peculiar argot and veterinary terms of their new language with only an occasional turn to the dictionary for the most obscure and technical words and phrases, such as "ear-candling." In addition to their natural talents, they worked constantly at it, to the detriment of their hygiene and the order of the house.

It is true that Vera's parents could be extremely distracted, and it was a good thing that they had a child who was responsible and not prone to criminal flights, for they would have no chance against a bad or sneaky child; she might sit in her room endlessly smoking her father's pipe, or take twenties out of her mother's purse to spend on chocolate, and they would never suspect a thing.

*Ear-candling is when you stick a paper tube in your ear and light it on fire to extract the ear wax. Surely unless you have a particular reason you want to go deaf, or must absolutely burn your hair off immediately, you might want to avoid it!*

As you can imagine, their jobs were not always filled with cheerful chatting about how to hold your cat still for eardrops (I have no idea how to do it myself!). Sometimes there were violent negotiations, and the translators had to be careful what they said. Often they were not working with language at all, but were forced to create meaning out of angry spittle. The trade agreement between the Hullocks and the Western Shives was hammered out in painful and prolonged circumstances, and both of Vera's parents had to have long courses of acupuncture to try and repair their health afterward.

Of course, I lied quite a bit when I said that Vera lived a completely average life. It was only that she didn't realize that it wasn't average, which meant that she didn't have all the facts, not that her view of things was incorrect. From the

*This is the scene on the third day of the trade talks, when things were still relatively genteel. Of course, if you are over ten, you remember the story of what happened in Week Two. It should have come as no surprise, anyway, that the passions involved were uncontrollable, and perhaps*

*the people involved might have prepared better for that. It is only natural that tempers will flare up when a culture tries to end a twelve-year embargo on the canned fish they need for their most beloved traditional holiday casserole.*

time she was born up until the present, they had lived one way. But the present was an utterly artificial moment, not in keeping with how her parents had lived so far, nor with how they or she would live in the future.

Before Vera was born, her parents' lives were fascinating, difficult, and sometimes even dangerous. They traveled to places on and off our world where the angry spilling of drinks was only a miniscule part of the difficulty and danger that they faced. You must ask them sometime to tell you about the April when they were called to a cave in the middle of a mountain to help in discussions with a famous warlord. These unusually tense negotiations were lightened by a flock of sheep who wandered in between the factions and could not be extracted except by a little boy with a feather duster who tickled them on their backsides.

Truth be known, Mr and Mrs Mironov preferred a certain degree of excitement in their professional lives. It was only because of Vera that they had lived this more sedate life in recent years.

Stationed in Moscow since Vera's birth, their work had been simple and cheerful: parties with dignitaries, catered lunches, and General Council meetings at the Jyptodome in Manezhnaya Square. Vera's parents got dressed each morning, drank coffee and ate croissants (juice and hand-fruit in addition for Vera, vitamins for all), dropped Vera at school, and went off to the UP arm in arm; her father, if the forecast said rain, tapping his umbrella cheerfully along the sidewalk.

Now all of this, going along as it was, would have been fine for Vera. She was not prone to the nail-biting, nervous behavior that her mother and father manifested when they had difficult work to do. She spent her time after school with her grandmother, cooking and listening to the radio until her parents got home. There were only a few nights that she could remember when her parents worked on letters until dawn and the coffee percolated in her dreams, for they were far from any interplanetary incidents in her early years.

Vera really knew very little about her parents' world as she packed her room into the green plastic crates that the shipping company supplied. The crates were to be stowed in the hold of a rocket ship, and then delivered from that rocket ship to their final destination by people who weren't even human, to a house that didn't look at all like a human house—at least not those you see most commonly on Earth: with level floors, flat panes of glass, and corners into which the dust can go.

She was leaving behind her grandmas and grandpas, her friends and teachers, her aunts and uncles and cousins, all familiar candy and bubblegum, radishes, spoons and tea, her family's little orange tree that sat in the front window of their apartment, the street that the apartment looked out on, her hamster, movie theaters, French fries, dogs, canaries and butterflies. She was leaving behind butter and flies as well.

And so, by the time Vera discovered herself on that rocket ship, the *Stephanie Cables*, she found that her excitement had mutated into a private, unchecked terror that she felt sure she must keep to herself. Mr and Mrs Mironov were good parents, and they would regret their decision if she told them how she felt. She did not want to cause them any grief. They were seasoned travelers, comfortable everywhere they went, but they sometimes did worry and bite their nails, and she could not bring on ulcers and eyestrain in people so far from their acupuncturist.

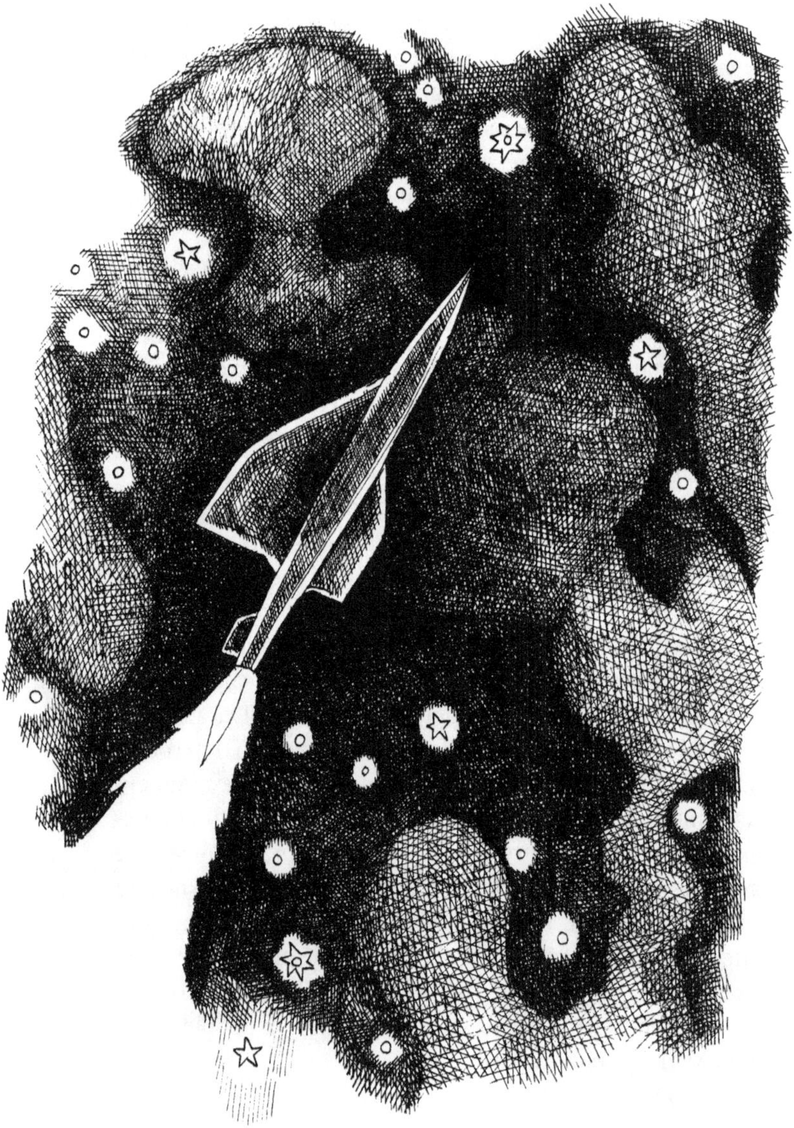

# V

HAVE you ever flown by rocket ship beyond the Black Magellanic Cloud? I suppose many of you have made your hops from here to there within our solar system, and those ships are very jolly and enjoyable, with silk-painting classes, well-stocked ice cream parlors, and acrobatics camp. But this flight was not really like that.

For one thing, the people on board were neither vacationing families nor retired cosmonauts who, from the comfort of the overstuffed armchairs on the viewing deck, wished to show their husbands and wives a little of what they had been missing over the years. All of the passengers were there for professional reasons. There were doctors, exozoologists, and a contingent of businesspeople from Nairobi who were hoping to sell artificial ivory to a manufacturer of musical instruments on Sobek. There were several groups of graduate students on their way to do field work, and three different groups from the United Planets: one in agriculture, one involved in the forging of trade agreements, and a third who were on what they referred to most vaguely as an "Expedition of Peace." They had brought along enormous trunks which they would visit frequently in the hold. That group drank heavily and did not like to talk shop.

It was a three-week flight, but beyond the bare minimum, there was little to do. The ship was outfitted for adults who knew how to entertain themselves, and the assumption was right. The travelers on board spent their hours with reading glasses on, gnawing up the backs of their pencils, studying flogged paperbacks filled with regional customs, and large tomes of alien flora and fauna. Many had never been to Sobek before, and some had never even met a Sobeki. All hoped that intense research would help them to avoid displays of bad manners, encounters with wild animals, and accidental poisonings.

Daily life was mostly quiet and professional aboard the *Stephanie Cables*. There were even extended reading hours in the public lounge. On another long-haul ship, this room might have been the site of thorough sing-alongs and various contests with peanut shells. Here, if you talked at all during these hours, you were pointedly shushed from all directions at once. This made things difficult for Vera; besides the public lounge, there was not a great deal of room for her to sprawl out.

Vera was the only child on board. This would have been an uncomfortable situation for any but the most asocial child, and Vera was very sociable. She would have taken up gladly with any child available to her. At home, she had friends older and younger, and with nothing better to amuse her, even a baby to chase after in the corridors would have brightened things up.

The youngest people on board were still ten years older than Vera at least. They were anthropology graduate students who had come as a group from the University of Minsk. The students were young, but the group was headed by an extremely old Finnish man named Tapio Koskinnen. He wore a bow tie and a neat beard, and had been going to Sobek for forty years—was in fact on the first Earth team to visit the planet. Though everyone on the ship would have liked to hear his stories, he did not like to tell them; in any language but

*Because of his early work in the field, Tapio Koskinnen (bottom right) is actually quite famous in Finland. You wouldn't know it by his quiet, unprepossessing air, but when he was a swashbuckling young man, any return to Earth was met by what the press called the "Koskinnen Krush," as the eligible set their caps for him. He himself hardly perceived the attention, and chose never to marry.*

Sobeki he had a pronounced stutter, and seemed somewhat self-conscious of it. He spent his time instead in the commissary, feet up, chatting with a Sobeki who worked there.

The graduate students that Koskinnen led were all from Earth—two young Russian women and two young American men. They had the look of backpackers who were late of the road, rangy and tan, though they were just now setting off. The men had beards and long hair, and the women wore their hair tied back in bandannas. They had brought all their things in ancient rucksacks, the enormous type that stretched above their heads and almost down to their knees. The backpacks barely fit in their cabins; they were big enough to sleep on if you got your positioning right.

The two women had been dating since college, and had developed a somewhat idiosyncratic way of talking between them. "Just wait," said Vera's father. "Couples who share field work become over-enmeshed. It is the eventual death knell of any relationship." As he spoke, he handed Vera's mother an orange that he had peeled and segmented for her. She accepted it without a thank-you, as if it had come from her own hand.

On discovering that the young women would share what food they had brought and were up for conversation, Vera spent a good deal of the trip shadowing them at their table in the commissary, or in their room sitting on those rucksacks and eating through their supplies. They seemed not to mind, and took Vera on as a little sister. Nadia, who was a gifted plaiter, went through her entire repertoire of braid styles on Vera's head, while telling her all she knew about Sobek. Nadia was studying fountain culture.

"The fountains in The Grand Bell have been in continuous

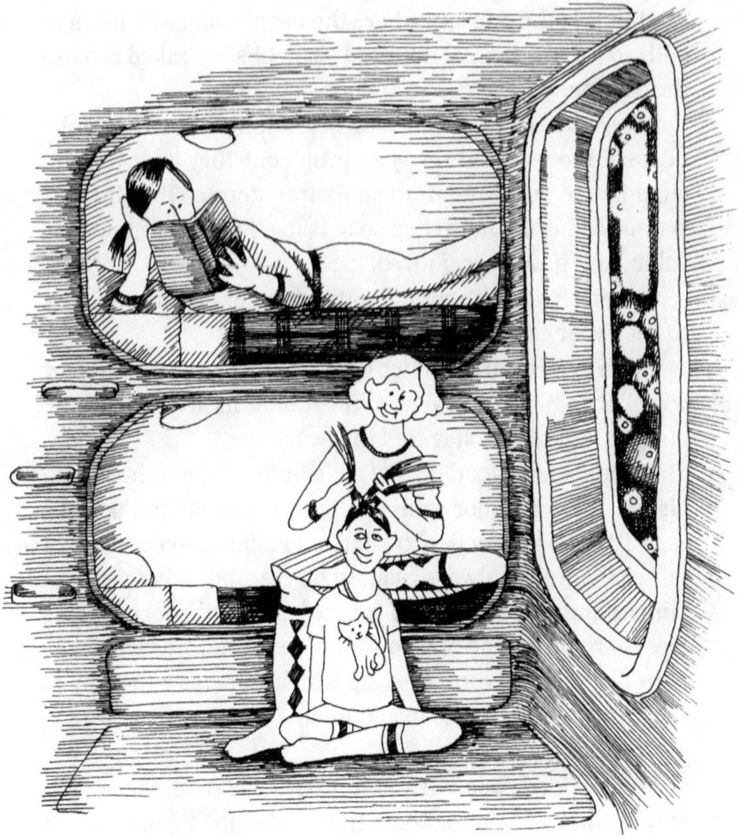

*Nadia attempts a very complicated "vernal twist" on Vera's hair, while Anja reads an especially unsettling murder mystery about an isolated research facility,* Bloodshed in Antarctica, *sent along by her mother.*

use since ancient times," said Nadia. "They are very beautiful, but it is the one city where the people all bathe in them still, so there's several hundred years of soap caked around the outside.

"There is a team of French preservationists coming on the next ship to work on the soap problem. They have been invited by the government to study it in depth. They haven't yet decided if the hardened soap is itself of anthropological value, or if it can be removed.

"I wish I hadn't cut my hair off. I think braids are very nice to keep your ears cool."

Anja looked up from her book. "Keep a wet cloth under your hat," she said to Vera. "The fountains are everywhere, and you will always stay cool that way."

"They spend a good deal of time in these fountains," said Nadia. "It is a major source of entertainment and socializing. It's not so practical by Earth standards—especially in our cities, we are always rushing places—but it is a very hot climate there, and taking a minute or two to cool off one's feet is an acceptable reason for lateness. In fact, Vera, they even have a one-word greeting which translates literally to the phrase 'Hello, I was in a fountain.'"

Vera laughed.

"Yes," added Anja. "If a family isn't in a rush, they might stay in the fountain for some time and enjoy themselves. It isn't unheard of to catch someone at an off-hour taking a little bath, though in many places it is now frowned upon to use soap." Vera listened and nodded with great interest, though she could not imagine the scene at all.

"When you first meet them," said Nadia, "I won't say it isn't surprising. They can look a little fearsome when you see a big group waiting in a train station. But you know, Vera, most of them have never seen an Earth person at all. At least on Earth we have lizards," she added, "so the look of them is not totally unfamiliar to us."

"But you really can't think of them as lizards," said Anja, looking up again from her book. Clearly she did not approve of this line of discussion. "They have a very highly evolved culture, and are really nothing at all like lizards. Even their internal organs do not correlate."

"I am only comparing their physiognomy. I am not some ignorant person calling them lizards." Nadia turned back to Vera. "Just as *we* find them peculiar, you mustn't be surprised if they stare at *you* when you go around."

"They're actually very mannerly," said Anja. "They won't really stare at you. But you know, when we were there several years ago they had a craze for wearing little wigs. There was an industrious old man who would sit in a park and weave these little hats out of the Murflus plant. It is a dark brown, hair-like plant that grows in tendrils. Many of them, and not just the children, were wearing those on their heads for a while."

"They loved to take pictures with us while wearing the wigs," said Nadia. "They would ask so politely, and really shake our hands with such appreciation afterward. You see, the only other type of person like us that they had seen were the Hoplocks, and you can imagine that that did not prepare them at all."

"I imagine the craze has worn off by now, though. It's extremely hot there for wigs."

As for the rest of the anthropologists, the two Americans, Bill and Walker, hadn't been to Sobek before. Like Vera's

*In the height of the craze, a good Murflus weaver could make and sell between ten and twenty wigs a day—wig and beard sets together, perhaps half that.*

parents, they kept their heads buried in books the entire trip except when they would stand up, unfurl their long frames, and demand a game of foosball from the nearest person.

They had prepared several weeks' worth of fudge, but they only brought it out after these games, so Vera always made sure to be present when the playing ended. They seemed to be very serious young men who were developing premature wrinkles between their eyes from their constant reading.

"The boys are nice, too," said Vera's mother as she ate her chicken paprika, "but the whole team seems the type to disappear into the capital city and never go back to Earth. Too serious! Watch: Twenty years from now, if you go back, you'll find Bill driving a tram, and the other one with his own juice business."

Vera's father tapped a boiled egg. He found the food in the cafeteria too salty, and for a week had eaten only eggs and fruit. "It's true," he said, looking up from the egg he was now poking in disgust. "People who engage in field work frequently lose their objectivity. The serious ones can snap.

"Look at how that boy Walker is hoarding all that fudge. He's extremely stingy with it for a boy who has about fifty boxes in his cabin," he said, decapitating his egg and pouring the yolk with disdain onto a waiting piece of toast. The uneaten fudge was even more irritating to him in the face of his plain and repeated meal. There was a Ukrainian who had been husbanding a large root of fresh horseradish throughout the trip, and Vera's father got up to see if he might be able to convince the fellow to grate a little on the side of his plate.

Vera's parents were busy trying to catch up on the last five thousand years of Sobeki culture, and had divvied up the books they intended to read, alternating histories and literature between the two of them. They seemed to be able to sit in a room indefinitely. When they rose at all, it was only due to medical necessity. At intervals, her mother would remind her father: "The veins, the veins. The blood will pool, dear."

Vera had her own intensive language program, complete with a workbook and headphones, and had much to learn beyond even the spoken language before she would really be able to communicate. Sobekis, who were extremely polite though they did not like to hold back their opinions, had a literal approach to subtext. They used a signing vocabulary in order to complement, amplify and undermine their speech. Vera had to learn that, too, for one could barely understand what they meant without it.

"It's the way they talk when what they have to say is too rude to say aloud," her mother explained. "They simply sign it discreetly. That way, they can deny it if they are caught out. Gesture is inadmissible in court."

"Yet there is no comprehensive dictionary for it," her father sighed. "I guess it falls to us to do it."

Vera had a fine attention span, but she was not like her parents. She left them frequently at the big tables in the common room to go walking around the ship.

"Check in frequently," said her father, looking up from *A Brief History of the North-Crenolat Renaissance.* "And if you can, bring me back a tea." Her mother looked up significantly from *A Time of Love: The Arboria Movement in Modern Verse.* "Yes, one for her, too," her father added.

The commissary was at the other end of the deck and was a decent walk, though there was nothing along the route to distract or entertain. The only possible entertainment had to come from the other passengers, since the portholes showed no view but the nighttime of space and the stars, and would not for a while. Lovely, very lovely, for a day or two, but after a week, only a faintly glimmering wallpaper.

Vera stopped by the game room to see if the foosball table was free. There was a game going on between a Dutch businessman and a Bolivian agronomist, and the line of people in folding chairs against the wall signaled the long wait time for the next game. After greeting those in the seats, and accepting thankfully a lollypop from Greta Freelander, a woman her parents knew vaguely from the UP, Vera continued on to the commissary.

The line there was always pretty bad, and though there was no charge, still you had to wait if you wanted hot water for tea, since the rocket ship could not have loose carafes of boiling water unsecured in the main room, in case of a gravity failure.

No matter how much one brought to do, inevitably one tired of it. You could see that by how quickly someone would offer to wait in line to buy a pack of gum for you, or run back to your room to retrieve a book—and of course, if given the key, they would take some time getting back, since they had been rummaging through your luggage and reading your diaries and letters.

At some point a passenger wanted to go to the park or the zoo, or to people-watch at a café, without seeing Marcus Hayashi, the businessman from Osaka, huffing past, doing his laps in the hallway.

Some of the passengers organized a bridge game that had now been in continuous play since the end of the first week, and you could find people playing at any time of day or night. Then there was a Mongolian man who gave a drawing class, setting up a nightly still life from the ephemera of people's luggage—nail clippers, paperback novels and loose change. For her part, Vera taught several passengers how to make friendship bracelets.

At the front of the line, stocking the candy trays behind the counter, was an old Sobeki man. He was the only alien on the ship, though Vera wouldn't have said that out loud. Her parents didn't like her to use such antiquated language.

He spoke no Earth language, and greeted customers with the same two-fingered salute and nod no matter how they greeted him. He chatted to everyone in Sobeki even if they didn't understand him, smiling and making change as if they were taking part in the conversation. Many of the passengers did know the language and responded in kind, but Vera was too shy even to make eye contact.

She often lingered nearby, listening in on his frequent conversations with Tapio Koskinnen, though she could make out nothing of their exchanges except that they enjoyed each other's company. The two spent a great deal of time laughing, Tapio Koskinnen guffawing heartily, and the Sobeki with a kind of piping bray. Vera longed to talk to him, though she didn't do it.

"Do you suppose he's about average height?" she asked her parents when she returned with their tea.

"Yes, he seems average from what I've read," replied her mother.

"And would you say that his voice is about average, too? It seems very gruff when he uses it."

"Well, he *is* an older man, you know."

"But who is he? Why is he here?"

"We've talked to him at great length," her mother said.

*Guilfoyle pours hot water into a container of instant pea soup, and considers his own plans for lunch.*

"He told us his whole life story once, while you were playing foosball with the scientists."

"Why don't *you* talk to him?" Vera's father said. "You know enough for a short conversation now."

"I can't understand him."

"Well, he calls himself Guilfoyle," said her mother. "He wanted to see the Grand Canyon, so he took a working passage. His wife refused to come with him, though, because she didn't want to leave the planet. She's afraid of hair. What else? He recently retired as a mailman, and this is his retirement present to himself."

"Do they have mailmen?"

"Yes, dear," said her mother. "You'll see many things that are the same, though in different form."

Vera thought suddenly of the mailman at home who had been so angry at her parents for taking her among the lizard people. Again, she squelched her desire to ask if they might develop a taste for human flesh. It was only some time later that she discovered that many Sobekis were ethical vegetarians who thought it was wrong to kill other animals for food. In fact, vegetarians made up an even greater proportion of the population than on Earth.

Now Vera thought of the spot behind the post office. She saw the gravel, and the loading dock where someone from the eighth grade had spray-painted a curse word. The parents had had a meeting about it. The curse word had been painted over, but you could still see the spot where it had been. There were many places in the neighborhood that she could picture perfectly when she tried to.

"How long are we staying?" she asked her parents. They looked up together.

"What do you mean, Vera? You know it's open-ended," said her father, with a mild look of irritation on his brow.

"We have to give it a chance," said her mother. "Adventures are sometimes even unpleasant, you know, but there is nothing better than having stories to tell. Even if you nearly go blind in a sandstorm, as long as you live through it, you'll find you're very popular at parties."

Vera did not find that at all reassuring.

"And Vera, you must begin preparing your talk for the Explorers Club. It will be very exciting. Perhaps they will give you another medal, or even a sash." Vera made an effort to smile at her mother, who added, "They have a delicious Beef Wellington, you know."

"Pssh," said her father, still with his eyes in his book. "That sauce was greasy!"

Vera laughed at that, and exchanged an amused look with her mother. Her father was an evangelical vegetarian, but though he pretended not to have tasted meat in years, he frequently sopped up gravy with his bread. The joke dissipated quickly, however, and by early evening, without even staying up for dinner, Vera had found her way to her bunk, where she fell asleep crying with Dasha's t-shirt over her head.

12
3
9
6

# VI

When an ocean liner makes a long journey across many time zones, the clocks are changed daily so that the passengers feel no discomfort. It's just the same on a rocket ship. When you travel on Earth, you must fly through darkness and light as you make your way around the world. On a rocket ship, of course, it is dark outside for the whole journey.

On the *Stephanie Cables*, the clocks were adjusted incrementally on a predetermined schedule. Every morning, the ship's steward made a cheerful announcement as to their plans for the day, clocks included. Three weeks was plenty of time to adapt to the new schedule, and the crew planned it so that the passengers would be on precisely the correct time when they got to their new destination. A vain undertaking, unfortunately, since things like the bridge game kept a large proportion of the passengers on random schedules of their own devising.

Nevertheless, they were inched closer to local time this way, as the ship sped through deep space. From within the cabins, there was no knowing the great distances they covered; as they pushed forward the hands of the clocks, those distances were converted to human scale. At the end of that immense black night, they descended to the planet of Sobek. Then, finally, they landed.

The passengers applauded the pilot. The pilot got on the loudspeaker to say something jolly, and the people on board, who had been packed and eager for several days, rolled their luggage down a gangplank and into a series of hermetically sealed rooms, and then finally into the fine and also hermetically sealed glass lobby of the Drift City Intersolar Spaceport.

The spaceport was both comfortable and well-appointed, like all but the most rudimentary establishments on the most backward planets have to be. People traveling from far away must stay in quarantine sometimes for quite a long while, depending on how rigid the local government is about germs. Whether the authorities judge the length of the quarantine by the incubation period of Ersatz Fever (thirty-six hours) or of Waldorf's Roseola (six weeks), they have the final word in all cases, and can keep you for as long as they want. In some places, your baggage has to stay even longer than you do, though you can see signs of corruption in spaceports that hold your possessions for more than a month and have many clothing shops in the quarantine area.

"The quarantine is absolutely necessary, Vera, so don't complain about it," said her mother when they were shown to their quarters by a team of hazmat-suited workers. "You wouldn't want a cold virus introduced that the population had never seen before. I don't suppose you want to be patient zero in a killing pandemic."

With only slight variations in their routine, the travelers continued on just as they had been going before. The same foosball rivalries continued in a game room that was much like the one on board the *Stephanie Cables*, and the same people queued up in the same order in the new commissary. But there was much more good cheer, and what variations there were to the routine felt thrilling. Now they all spent a great deal of time in the garden sniffing the peppery fragrance of the Dinner Rose. For hot water, they could now serve themselves, from an urn that was minimally secured.

The meals in the cafeteria were much better here, since a truck dropped off fresh fruits and vegetables to an airlock at the back of the port every morning. The cafeteria even employed a cook from Earth, a man named Luce, with a cheerful yellow beard that he wore in a hairnet. He had moved to the planet a few years before, and found his skills in high demand. He liked to make flapjacks every morning, and had trained a galley of young Sobekis in the art form, which they did behind glass. There could be no physical contact with the Earthman, and though there was an intercom, Luce was always too busy to talk. "See you on the outside!" he'd say to them through the intercom. "Hope you liked the flapjacks!"

The view out the window was of a vast desert, unchanging beyond a surface rippled by the wind and the light of the sun moving across the sand. The windows were tinted to cut the glare, which was clearly considerable, as the few times they saw workers outside they were wearing large, dark goggles.

For a mass of people who had been traveling in deep space for several weeks, the featureless desert was endlessly interesting. Vera and the anthropologists sat and stared out into the waste for hours at a time. Once in a while, a long-eared creature that looked quite a bit like the rabbits of Earth would come and stop at the window to admire its reflection in the mirrored glass. At each appearance of these little animals—Pupu, as Tapio Koskinnen called them—crowds of the quarantined clustered around and cheered enthusiastically. The animals delighted them all, and were the bright spot of their day inside the spaceport.

"Hooray! Hooray for Pupu!" shouted the serious-minded businesspeople and academics, some hopping up and down.

"Youpi!" "Ypa!" "Hurra!" "Hao wa!" and etc., in all the languages present.

Vera's parents could not be lured by Pupu. They continued their studies as if they hadn't landed.

"Aren't you curious?" Vera asked them. "Don't you want to see what's out there?"

"Of course," said her father, "but we must see to our duties. You know the ambassador has been without a translator for months."

Vera did not particularly need their attention; there was a good deal more to see and do in the spaceport than there had been to see and do in space. Vera was fascinated by the workings of the spaceport.

If you've traveled in space before, you know that there are many things that you are not supposed to bring with you; it is much more regulated than when you travel from country to country on Earth. Even children can probably list the things you can't transport, but some adults get it into their heads to carry whatever they like, regardless of the sensible rules. Of course, it is hard not to stuff your pockets full of alien seeds to take home, I agree, as your aunt would really appreciate the gift, and further, how will you know if the soil is hospitable unless you try planting them? Yet the urge must be resisted!

You will find that Sobeki customs officers like it no better than Earth customs officers when you try to bring in alien seeds, and obviously you'll get nowhere at all with that log of salami. Just as on Earth we have specially trained dogs who sniff certain things out, on Sobek they employ small goatish creatures called "shopmen" who travel in little packs around the spaceport and are even more effective at discovering your contraband than the most adept German shepherd. This too

*This shopman is pleased to have discovered an especially garlicky sausage brought from a famous Warsaw deli, but will be regretting it in an hour or two when he is forced to lie down for a while in a cool corner of the arboretum until the heartburn passes.*

created endless amusement for the quarantined, and Vera especially, who watched out for their arrival gladly, and fed them flapjacks each morning from her breakfast.

Some of them had grown very plump from the scraps, and greedy, too, such that when they were offered no leftovers, they would muscle past each other into the arboretum and gobble up whatever fruit from the trees had fallen to the ground there. Vera had even seen a particularly plump one chomp down on a clod of loamy earth that it had knocked over itself from a low shelf in the arboretum. Vera was reminded of an obese cat who lived in an ice cream parlor near her house in Moscow. The cat would jump up on the tables and lap up all the melted ice cream and fudge detritus from the bowls before they could be cleared by the waitress. The shopmen were just as bad as that, and they had no handler at all to control them. They did not like creatures outside of their own breed, and without question, they would not have obeyed a handler, anyway.

After a week the doctors cleared them all to leave, and the shopmen cleared their luggage. What sign the doctors had been waiting for wasn't clear, but there was one last temperature reading, and then the Sobeki doctors in their hazmat suits shook their hands and said cheerfully, "See you on the outside! You're healthy and free to go!"

The shopmen had pulled out the last sweets and noodles from their bags. They had declared their luggage clean and clear by simply losing interest, for as the week passed, they sniffed around less and less, gnawing one final corner off a leather bag to get at a crumb or two, and then moving on to greener pastures, which meant hanging around en masse by the kiosks while sandwiches were being made.

Cleared from quarantine, the passengers walked outside a few at a time, until they were all gathered on the far side of the airlock, and faced with the land beyond the spaceport. They had been together for a full month, and it was not easy to leave each other's sides and get on with their real business. Even those who had been the most standoffish pulled each other's ears and poked their neighbors affectionately.

There was much hugging and kissing and exchange of little trinkets. Business cards were passed from hand to hand with private messages written on the backs, and everybody posed for snapshots in the bright sunlight. But finally, after the last hand had been shaken and the last card exchanged, they were forced to admit it was time to part. Some hopped onto the enormous buses queued up in front of the terminal, or found the Sobeki hosts who were waiting for them outside. One or two of them simply walked off down the dusty street, though the next town was many miles away.

"Stretch my legs!" said Maurice Hayashi, the businessman from Osaka who ran every day, as he sprinted off happily, having sent his luggage on ahead.

The anthropologists were due back to another area of the spaceport for a local flight on a somewhat ragged airplane that was resting on its haunches just outside on the runway. The city they were going to was on the other side of the world from where Vera was staying. The Sobekis, though they were as proficient as anyone in space, had not worked out the details of air travel at all. Their planes were all at least fifty years old, and jarring to the nerves. Their flight attendants had a policy of giving out stiff drinks to all on board—children included—before taking off, and their union had discussed, but later tabled, a proposal to flood the cabins with a gentle soporific gas at ten-minute intervals throughout the flights.

"Goodbye, my dear little sister," said Nadia. "We will miss you." And they all hugged and shook hands. "We will see you again, if not here then back on Earth."

"Oh, but she will be a grown-up when we see her again," said Anja, and wiped her eyes. Guilfoyle, who was going to the same part of the world as they were, waited by the luggage with Tapio Koskinnen and the Americans. As Vera left with her parents, they blew one last kiss to her, and she did not even feel foolish, but caught it as she always had with her grandmother, and pressed the kiss eagerly to her cheek.

## VII

OUTSIDE, waiting for the Mironovs with his body in the shade of a thin, leafy tree and his tail warming in the sunlight, stood a rather young-looking Sobeki holding a large sign in Russian. He looked up at all the hub-bub, and soon approached them with a smile.

"Sent from the embassy," said the little note card that he pulled out of his purse. "Please come with me, and I will take you to your new home." He did not speak Russian at all, and was very glad to discover that Vera's parents spoke Sobeki. He seemed not to have expected it, though he knew, of course, that they were translators.

"That's certainly a relief," he said, "though I have many fine conversations where I only smile and nod. There's sack lunch in the cart, and your luggage will be sent ahead."

"That is very cordial of the ambassador."

"No, not at all. The lunches are from me alone. The ambassador told me not to bother."

"Really?"

"'Not in the budget,' he said. Your planet must be very poor indeed, for all I made you were fish sandwiches, purple salad, and a little chocolate pudding. It put me out only eight krucks toner fifty." He shrugged and led them to their ride.

Before them on the street lay a large animal sprawled on its side in the hot sun, and looking for all the world like a giant dog, waiting for its stomach to be scratched.

The Sobeki introduced himself as Alfonse. "That's what the ambassador likes to call me, as he can't pronounce my

*Alfonse goes out of his way to project style and job mobility. He has all his hats made at a specialty haberdasher at the edge of the city. They keep a mold of his foremost ridge on a shelf at the back for his future orders.*

name, though I've taken to it, to be honest. I think it suits me, and I find your letter 'f' very amusing."

He made several whistling sounds, did indeed scratch the animal's stomach for a moment, and then, pleased by the attention and taking its own time, the animal rolled itself up to a sitting position. Alfonse offered it a green ball about the size of a large grapefruit, and the animal sniffed at it delightedly and pressed it with its tongue. The ball was made up of fresh leaves wrapped tightly and covered in a sticky substance, and Alfonse had a small bag over his shoulder that was full of them. The animal closed its eyes in a display of placid relish as it ate, licked its lips, and then sat calmly waiting for them.

"They are very nice," Alfonse said, "and tolerate us on their backs. You mustn't hit them in any way, though, or pinch them, or anything like that. They will throw you right off, and step on you, too, and then when they've pressed you to the ground, bite your foot off."

"That doesn't sound very nice," said Vera's mother, who hesitated to translate what the Sobeki had said for Vera.

"Oh, tell her," said Vera's father. "That way she will know how to avoid getting her foot bitten off."

Behind the enormous animal, Alfonse attached a little cart that was big enough, but barely, for Vera and her family. It looked like the sort of cart you might see hitched to a mule in the country, and in fact, it had even been filled with something like straw as a shock absorber.

"The ambassador's wife thought it might be too soon in your stay for you to ride on top of the footslog. She suffered from bad vertigo on her first attempt. They do sway a bit, though I suppose if you'd like to try, I could tie you on. I know

*The footslog carries riders graciously, unless pushed to the limit.*

a few very good knots."

Vera's parents waved the idea away. "The cart will do just fine," said Vera's mother. "Very nice of her to send us one."

It *was* very nice, after so long in hermetic rooms, to feel the breeze and smell the clean air as they traveled along. Even sneezing had a certain pleasure, as there had not been an allergen or living particle in the air they had been breathing for the last month. They had grown used to the smell of plastic and the coal odor of the filters, sometimes covered by the good smells of cooking and the passengers' hand lotions, but it had been a vaguely unpleasant background to their trip.

The landscape passed quickly as the creature loped along, and the strange creeping plants and undulating hillocks flew by. "Footslog" was not at all a fitting name for it, and Vera and her parents wondered about its origins.

Alfonse had set up an awning for them so they wouldn't be out in the hot sun, but he sat atop the animal in the open very cheerfully, and seemed not to mind the heat. Every so often, he called down to see if they were all right.

"Hello!" he said. "Do you like the pudding?"

"Yes, yes," they replied. "Delicious!" He had left a bottle of water with the Mironovs in the cart, and they finished it quickly, finding that they were very thirsty even though they weren't sweating. It was clear that a Sobeki wouldn't naturally know how much water a human would need, as they needed much less themselves.

"One must take special care not to get dehydrated in the desert," Vera's father said, popping a tablet from a little vial of UP Hydration Supplement (Human/Desert) and handing it around.

Soon they were on the outskirts of a small city at the edge

*The tram system does not appear to be a practical choice for a desert city, but it generates a delightful breeze as it passes.*

of that large, arid waste, rolling next to tracks that seemed to have emerged from the sand of the desert. A tram appeared from around the corner, and the footslog raised its head, and from its throat issued a cordial, hooting cry, as though it were familiar with the creature. The tram kept pace with the footslog for several blocks, then rang its bell and pulled ahead. The footslog responded in kind, as if to say goodbye, and continued on its way.

The mass transit system was made up of trams just like the ones you find on Earth. It was a technology quite common in that part of the galaxy. The sidewalks were cobbled in small, shiny stones, but the streets were not paved. Every time a tram came by, a cloud of dust was blown around in its wake. The footslogs wore hats that covered their ears, and each had some sort of eye protection, but still they whinnied when the dust hit them, as if they were expecting it to bother their eyes even when it didn't.

The silken face masks and goggles of the footslogs were a comical sight, but the animals wore their accessories proudly; the more ornate the head-covering, the more happily they trotted. They did not even object to having things pasted to their faces. Vera's mother poked Vera to point out the animal fashions as they passed.

"Look at that capelet!" said Vera's mother. "I wonder how they get them to hold still while dressing them."

The houses and buildings soon began to appear in clusters, like fruit on a branch. One could get the impression from looking at it that the city had grown organically, blooming off of the avenues. Then they were in Drift City, in the southernmost precinct of the Collection of Small Municipalities. It was the capital of that area. The size did not suggest

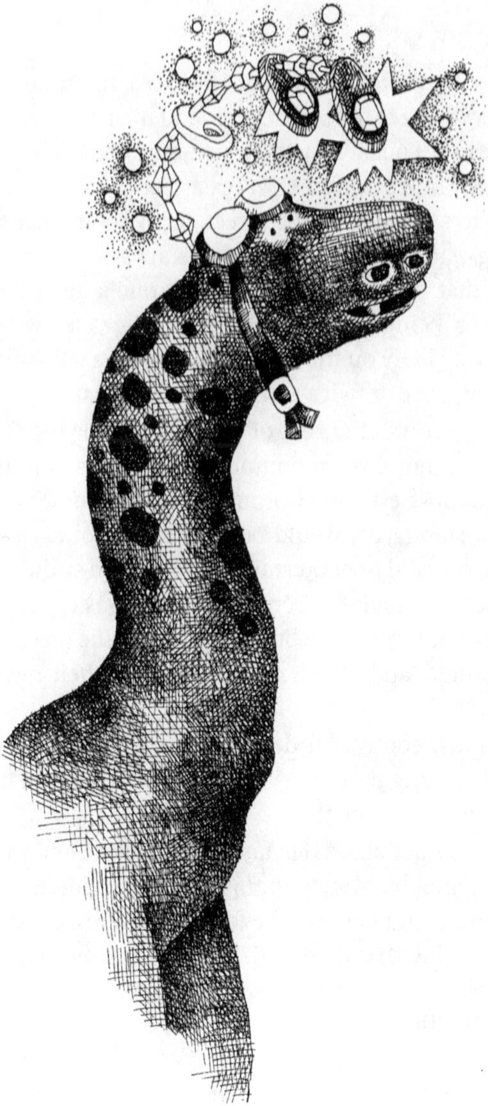

*This splendid footslog was so enamored with his own glittering headgear that he stopped in the middle of a busy thoroughfare to admire it, causing inconvenience and delay for everyone else on the road.*

its status, for the Sobekis did not like great metropolises, and kept everything to the scale they found most pleasant. Rarely did cities on Sobek grow to a size that made it difficult to know everyone's name, or at least recognize everyone well enough to say hello on the street. They took great stock in greetings, and the government was always commissioning studies that proved definitively that one's good health depended on being greeted at least five times a day by name, and kissed gladly on the cheeks by someone who was happy to see you, once or twice a day at the very least.

Though it was the seat of government for the CSM, the Sobekis did not favor monumental buildings, and they put even the most esteemed branches of government in what, by Earth standards, would be considered cottages. By convention, they did not entertain formally, and so did not need state rooms or halls. When the weather was especially nice, visiting dignitaries were brought to a specific picnic ground for meetings, and were expected to carry their own picnic baskets.

"We must control all despots," said the writings of the CSM's founding parents, "by making sure they do not have private swimming pools."

They did not share our taste for columns and marble in governmental buildings, though they considered marble to be beautiful, and many of the fountains were carved out of it. The only thing that distinguished judges from other professionals was that they wore flower wristlets which they sniffed frequently. The official purpose of the flowers was to remind the judges to stay calm, though of course, Sobekis are just like anyone, and they did not maintain noticeably better spirits, even with their official flowers on.

The city that Vera and her parents were entering seemed empty at first, for it was the height of the day, and just the wrong time for pedestrians. The Mironovs couldn't see many of the buildings well, as the city was made up of a network of interconnected gardens protected from the sand that surrounded them by high walls. The walls were not intended for privacy, and no visitors were discouraged by them. Neighbors did not require an invitation to walk into each other's gardens. This hospitality and ease was not visible from the street, though; the high walls concealed all but the tops of the trees and the roofs of the houses.

"Here we are," said Alfonse, dismounting from his footslog before it had gotten down on its knees. With a flourish, he slid down its leg, and gave the animal another leaf ball from his bag. The animal laid down to gnaw on it, eyes closed in the sun.

He had brought them up to the gate of their new house. The home itself rose from the sand and looked a part of it, which it was, carved from the soft rock that jutted out of the land. Except for the holes cut into the sides—its modest windows—and the flowered café curtains fluttering just behind them (someone had done their best to make the place cozy for Earth people), at first glance it might have been a strange desert vision, uninhabited save for the light of the moon and the sun, and the small animals that used its shade.

Vera did not notice the groomed flower bushes around it, nor the care with which someone had laid stone paths to the front door and through the surrounding garden. The building looked only like a strange rock formation, in which one might be imprisoned by magic.

Nature comes up with many such things, like the eerie

*As the family will soon discover, the ground floor of the house remains cool, but at the height of day, the top of the building gets hot and uncomfortable, like a big sore thumb sticking out of the landscape.*

statues that rise from salt lakes on our own Earth. But the fact that Earth too produces strange forms was no consolation for Vera. On Earth, one did not generally make one's home in the middle of a salt lake.

"It's homey," said Vera's mother as they stood on the walk outside of the building. She patted her daughter on the back. Vera did not respond. Vera's mother said it again in Sobeki to Alfonse, who agreed with a great smile on his face.

"Oh, I do think so," he said most sincerely.

"It's as homey as a disembodied claw," said Vera's father in Russian. Despite his profession and place of work, he sometimes uncontrollably said what was on his mind.

His quip made Vera and her mother laugh. Alfonse, who hadn't the slightest idea what Vera's father had said, for no one had translated it, in any case laughed along with them most cheerfully.

## VIII

FIRST nights in new houses are usually jarring. One can lie in bed for hours, taking the measure of the smells, the creaks and the currents of the breeze as it moves through the rooms. But on this first night, the Mironovs were so tired that they fainted immediately into the soft beds that Alfonse had prepared, and slept dreamlessly. They would have slept as well in a sandy ditch if it had been offered up to them. They didn't take off their shoes; nor did they brush their teeth, and Vera's parents were most particular about their teeth, so that was really saying something. Vera's father, especially, would take to his gums for quite some time after meals.

"Life is often uncontrollable," Vera's father had told her repeatedly, "so you must be sure to manage those things that you can."

Vera's parents were usually early risers. Her father maintained that he had never slept past seven in his life, but many were the New Year's Days that Vera and her mother had seen him sacked out until noon, on the couch and snoring. There had been other occasions as well. He needed eight hours, and would make it up somehow if he missed it at the beginning of the night. On this day, the family, early risers though they might have been, would have slept all day without an alarm clock, but they were awakened to a bustling excitement downstairs about an hour before dawn.

"Ludicrous!" said her father, still asleep. "The middle of the night is no time for a riot."

"We have burglars!" shouted Vera's mother, although she shouted it very quietly so as not to alert the source of the noise.

"Rats! Desert rats!" bellowed Vera's father, who was now fully awake and no longer in a misty dream about friendly rioters. "They will eat our only child!" Then he grabbed the leg of a chair that he found lying beside the bed, and headed to the stairs. As for Vera, she woke to the suggestion that she would soon be eaten and, quaking behind her parents, headed after them.

They could see the entire lower floor from the top of the stairs. Down in the center of the room stood a group of three Sobekis hovering over a sheet of paper. They seemed to be in the act of setting up the dining room table. They consulted the instructions, then put the last nails into the supports. After that, they placed a large cake on top, poured themselves glasses of what looked like lemonade, and sat down around it on packing crates. The chairs had not been set up yet, as witnessed by the fact that Vera's father was holding a leg from one of them.

Vera's parents scuttled back to their bedroom to confer. "It seems cheerful enough, but it might simply be a ruse to put us at our ease. Perhaps they are lying in wait?" said Vera's mother. "We mustn't be fooled by the presence of a cake. Don't you remember that folk tale about the sand plover and the mustard?"

"Yes, yes. I'm certain of it," said Vera's father. "Your instincts are good. Did you see that one lustily pouring drink down his throat? Who knows how long he's been running this racket. He's seasoned, well-seasoned. I want you and Vera to climb out the window. It's not very high and you'll fall right into the sand if you jump accurately. Watch out

*Vera and her parents quake at the top of the stairwell as they watch the nefarious Sobeki strangers put together a table, possibly as a site for a human sacrifice.*

for the bush! Then run as fast as you can to the ambassador's house. I'll hold them off."

Vera's mother scowled. "You can just as easily climb out the window with us as hold them off. Why risk yourself simply to save our belongings?"

"I suppose you're right," said Vera's father, reconsidering. "Let's go together, then. I'll jump first, and you can throw Vera down to me." They stood there for quite some time in the upstairs bedroom, deep in conversation, while the intruders at the table downstairs chatted and drank their juice. Perhaps it was malevolent chatting and drinking of juice, but to an outside observer, it really did not seem that way. It seemed that way to Vera and Vera's parents, however, all three of whom had been awakened from a sound sleep.

"Here goes nothing," said Vera's father, adjusting his position on the sill. Then he offered up what appeared to be a silent prayer and jumped out of the window onto the sand. He made no noise but a smothered groan as he landed, and lay clutching his ankle on the ground. Later he was quite proud of his restraint in not shouting out, and remarked on many occasions to Vera's mother that he could act stoically and keep his wits about him even in great danger. "I've been tested, and it's true: I'm not lacking."

"At least I missed the bush," he said. "From down here you can really see the thorns. Let me catch my breath, and then you two jump down onto me. I'm no good to you anymore. Jump and run; I can't follow you. I've hurt my ankle." Vera's mother took him at his word, and was just about to throw Vera down onto her father—though Vera protested a little, unsure why she could not just jump—when one of the individuals from downstairs poked a head out the front door.

*Vera's father tries to put on a brave face from his dire position flat on his back in the sand.*

"Hell-ooo!" he called to Vera's father. "Family Mironov, father of the family, what are you doing in the sand, lying there like that?" he said in extremely broken Russian. Vera's father could not easily muster a threatening and authoritative tone from his position on the ground, but he tried.

"Quick, Anfisa! Throw me down the chair leg!" Vera's mother stayed where she was and did not go get it, so Vera's father carried on with his prostrate display. "Why are you in our house? I demand an explanation!"

The man on the doorstep smiled and replied in Sobeki, "Let me help you into the house. I am 'Norbert Wiener,' the mayor of Drift City. We are simply the welcoming committee! We have brought you a cake and traditional juices. It is nothing more menacing than that, my friends."

Vera's father sighed. "The mayor, indeed." He accepted the Sobeki's arm, and was lifted out of the sand. Sobekis are extremely strong and can lift even a man of Vera's father's size very easily. There is a story that has circulated over the years of an air crash, and a Sobeki who carted a human across the Sere Flats for hundreds of miles with only one canteen of water to drink, though perhaps it is only folklore, since so many claim to have taken part.

"I wanted us all to wear wigs so that you would feel more at home, but both 'Barthes' and *Gerullup, gerullup!* thought it was a bad idea. Well, I didn't agree with them, but it was two against one." Now the mayor looked up and saw Vera and her mother still hanging out of the window.

"Hell-ooo!" he said to them. "Come down and eat cake! We are so eager to talk to you. We love Earth people. Oh, we don't meet very many of them.

"And you know, I have never seen a child in person. I see

you are blessed with the hair that all of your species wears," he said to Vera, peering up at her in the window. "I suppose I thought that it came in later."

After the Mironov family settled themselves at the table and recovered somewhat from their primarily self-induced scare, the mayor's staffers poured each of them a tall glass of pulpy juice.

The mayor then continued. "I will tell you, I can count on two hands my humans. There was Jackie Schubert. You look quite a bit like her. She had ears, too, you know, and that sort of nose and chin you have. And hair, of course. Just a little bit like that, all over her head and coming around her face. Like the mane of the Hahaplunks, right?" He turned to his aide *Gerullup, gerullup!* "Do you see the resemblance?"

"To the Hahaplunk mane? Well, theirs goes all around their face under their chin," she gestured. "Mr Mironov has it, but these two are quite bald there."

"I suppose so. I'm not as observant as I might be."

"Her hair was also blonde and curly, not dark."

"Oh, no," said the mayor. "The hair is the same." *Gerullup, gerullup!* shook her head.

"Suit yourself," said the mayor, a little peeved to be corrected publicly.

"I asked the ambassador to come over," said the mayor, "but he said he never rises earlier than Clotchnok, which is the lunch bell. What a lazy fellow!"

"It's not the case," said Barthes. "He wakes up at dawn. I suppose it pains him to greet anyone or say 'Hi, how are you.' And he absolutely won't come and share a cake with the neighbors. He doesn't eat cake."

"No!" said the Mayor. "What a monstrous ninnyhammer,

pardon the expression! Well, he is no asset to a party, that much is certain. We're better off without him. His lovely wife is another story, but she's out of town presently."

He turned and looked seriously at Vera's family. "But you three do not look up for it at all."

"Well, we don't usually have our parties just at dawn," said Vera's father, laughing.

"No?" said the mayor. "Though it's tradition, it's also my own predilection—the loveliest time of day, after all. When the sun rises, we will go outside to salute her with a song." The mayor stood and sang:

> Madame the Sun, how you warm my belly and
>   my knees.
> My toes appreciate the warmth of the soil,
> To say nothing of my nether regions and the root
>   of my tail.

Vera and her parents tried to hum along once they'd caught the tune, but it was hard going, and they stopped to listen after a moment.

"Very nice, mayor," everyone said.

Barthes turned to the Mironovs and said cheerfully, "He really has a lovely voice. It's why he was elected. He sang his campaign song, and wrote it, too. It made his opponent look very prim, as she had no song herself. Not the best electoral politics, but you know, the voters can be quite superficial." He shrugged. "We made sure he sang it at every one of his campaign stops."

The mayor's entourage was a cheerful bunch. He was not the only one who liked to sing and cut up. *Gerullup, gerullup!* brought out a little flute and began to play a tune, and the

*Before he went into politics, the mayor pursued vocal training quite seriously, and was known by his teachers for having a voice that "cool[ed] and refresh[ed] the spirit like an entire afternoon spent in a well-regulated fountain."*

group got to their feet and did a series of cheerful dances in the round. The dances were easier to catch than the songs since the Sobekis were loose and unhurried in their movements. They did a great deal with the presentation of their hands, and somewhat less with footwork.

The mayor took some time dancing with Vera's mother, and then her father, and then with Vera, each in their turn. It was a custom in that part of the world that everyone in a room should dance with everyone else, even babies and the very old. Things became complicated when babies were supposed to dance with babies, but they had a procedure to cover that. These traditions meant that a large party could go on for quite some time, and those who had to leave early could be seen making their way through the assembled revelers with a businesslike expression on their faces as they danced.

The mayor was a courteous dancer, and concluded each dance with a kiss on his partner's cheek. Vera had never felt the skin of a Sobeki before. It was very cool and smooth, and his hands were quite a bit softer than she had expected. Up close, the mayor smelled wonderful, like fresh grass, and for a long time afterward, Vera believed that Sobekis smelled unlike any human or animal on Earth. Later she learned that it wasn't their natural smell, but a very nice beauty product, somewhere between a soap and a lotion, a bit like a saddle soap, that many of them used to keep their thick reptilian skin in good form. When Vera finally discovered the source, she and her mother sent her grandmother and aunts a big box. All who used it appreciated it very much for rubbing onto their dry heels.

Though they had been woken from a sound sleep and terrified, it was true that a morning party had its charms. The blue light of dawn turned slowly into sunshine, and a morning breeze wafted through the open windows.

The aides set to work in the kitchen and prepared a big breakfast with supplies they had brought along for the purpose. This, they informed Vera, was a good deal of their job. "What else would it be?" Barthes asked. "The mayor prefers to do the paperwork himself."

Though neither Vera nor her parents could identify any of the ingredients, it was a delicious meal seasoned with a mild onion—perhaps made of mushrooms, perhaps chick peas, they could not tell. Vera's father did not inquire as to what he was eating, and asked for seconds with great cheer.

After breakfast was done and the dishes were washed, the mayor leaned back cheerfully in his seat, which was a box of books that barely accommodated his rump and tail.

"Do you know," he said, picking his teeth with the stem of a flower from a bouquet that sat on the table, "though I am enjoying this party so much and am very glad to finally meet you all, my heart is not as light as it appears. We have a most alarming situation with our fountains. The worst problem I've faced this term. An invasive species is taking over and clogging the drains, and it's causing quite a lot of spillover into the squares. And Vera," he said, turning to her, "how do you think they are entering the fountains?" Vera, who had remained quiet for much of the morning, didn't know.

"No guess? Any of the Earth people?"

"We have this on Earth," said Vera's mother, "if people don't clean off the bottoms of their boats when they transfer them between bodies of water, but I don't imagine there are boats that go in your fountains."

"Well," said the mayor, "we do have toy boats, of course.

These are public fountains, after all. But the toy boats aren't the problem."

"Perhaps they come through the water supply?"

"No, not at all," said the mayor, and he raised his hand to stop them in case anyone had the intention of guessing again. "We have very nice, thick toes, you see, very attractive, æsthetically pleasing." He suddenly seemed to regret bragging to the gathered Earth people, and added, "I'm sure you have very nice toes, too, though you hide them so. It does make one wonder what's the matter with them."

"They're very sensitive," said Vera's father. "They can't comfortably walk on rocks and all that without some form of covering."

"No? Well, you are a spongy people, I've noticed. That skin of yours is a strange evolutionary cul de sac. I really wonder over it sometimes. I do fear for its integrity. One might poke through it so easily. May I?" He grasped Vera's father's hairy arm and poked it gently with his claw.

"Well, good, it doesn't break through as easily as that. And at least you have this handsome fur all over. That must help."

"I suppose it does something," said Vera's father, "if you have it." The Mayor put down Vera's father's arm reluctantly and continued.

"We have very beautiful feet. But this season a strange and disturbing fashion has taken hold among some of the smart set. On their vacations in the mountains, they have begun wearing shoes in the water. I fear this fashion actually comes from the influence of your planet. And why those who have no need would take on the correctives of those with a physical disability, I will never know."

*Actually the mayor had poked Jackie Schubert's forearm on several occasions—they were very close—but had not thought it a generally representative limb.*

Thinking that he simply said the truth, the mayor did not apologize for his words, nor did he even notice that he might have. "The treads on these hideous things are very deep to make stepping on stones easier—totally unnecessary for us, in fact actually impeding, for we are very sure-footed, especially those of us who live in the Northern Mountains past Klonbarg. These very deep treads allow shrimp eggs from the lakes to gather in the crevices. And then these foolish individuals bring the eggs home to our fountains. As you might guess, they, like the dunderheads they are, wear the shoes in the fountains where they could have no possible reason for them. Even human visitors see no need for that! Jackie Schubert would bathe twice a day, and I never saw her wear shoes inside a fountain. If you have not seen them yet, they are built so the bottoms are not very slippery. So you see, this is how the shrimp arrived. They have been breeding endlessly, and now they are spilling out of the fountains."

"They skitter around on the stones and sun themselves," said *Gerullup, gerullup!* "They seem eager to relocate even beyond the fountain, in fact, though it's hard to know their real intentions. We have employed several people to try to contain them with brooms."

"Is that working?" asked Vera's mother. She used to keep plants on their fire escape at home, and was always fighting off neighborhood cats with a broom when they came for her tomatoes.

*Gerullup, gerullup!* shook her head. "Only temporarily," she replied.

"Are we in danger? The fountains aren't poisoned with venom, are they?" asked Vera's father, who sometimes became nervous when faced with smaller animals, insects or microbes, and certainly wanted to know before they went in whether he and his family should avoid the fountains. "Are they biting the little children?"

"The inconvenience alone is enough. One can hardly find a place to put down one's tail," the mayor said. "If you run into Jangletown folk who seem dustier than usual, you must be understanding. Some have even given up bathing entirely! They are completely besieged.

"Here, I have a picture. I carry it with me to remind myself and others what we are up against." He brought out a snapshot of a shrimp from his purse. The shrimp looked precisely like the ones we have on Earth, and stared soulfully into the camera with its goggle eyes. "You see, they have a somewhat fearsome visage," said the mayor without irony.

"Our problem is two-fold," said Barthes, as though he were reading back from the agenda. "First we must convince folks not to wear shoes. And then we have to get rid of the shrimp. It's a true quagmire," he sighed.

"Those shod scofflaws are offended that we're singling them out and blaming the problem on them," said the mayor. "They do not want to give up their shoes. I'm afraid to imagine what other clothes they will wear next season, and what other environmental disasters they will cause consequently. Why they cannot simply enjoy their bodies unencumbered I will never understand. Why cover your toes? It can only breed bacteria."

"How will you remove the shrimp?" asked Vera's father, who was becoming a bit agitated at the thought of an incipient slaughter.

"We will catch them with nets, I suppose. I can't imagine what else. Not with our hands; they're pretty quick. Is there

*The shrimp, or bile fish as it's called locally, has several other survival techniques beyond just inedibility.*

another way I haven't considered? Perhaps you have a tool on Earth created especially for shrimp invasions?" he inquired eagerly.

"What will you do with them once you catch them?" asked Vera's father.

"Unfortunately, they are not tasty at all," said the mayor. "They are extremely bitter, in fact, because of the way they process their waste. In the north they call them [he gave a high, discordant whistle]."

Vera's mother whistled back to him questioningly. He nodded, and she said to Vera, "The word is 'bile fish.'"

"We will drive them by truck back into the mountains, what else?" The mayor shrugged. "Huge waste of time and money. If people will only take them for home terraria, we could save a million koblanks." The mayor sighed. "It's the sort of budget killer I hoped not to run into this season. We already have our hands full with several important initiatives. Not to mention the school year will be starting soon. The schools have budgeted an impossible number for gardeners, and all have claimed the same year that the Loblolly balls are flat and need to be replaced. As I'm sure you know, those are unconscionably expensive."

He took a sip of juice and settled down. "We made up posters to warn the public about the shrimp, and we have to get them up somehow. We pay volunteers if you would like to do it," he added, turning toward Vera.

"Maybe Vera can do it in a week or two when she's more comfortable," Vera's mother said.

"Well, I don't suppose the problem will be cleared up in a week or two, but we will try."

# IX

THE translators' residence was a modest bungalow set in the same small park as the ambassador's. The senior diplomat's house was not much less modest than the junior; it was only slightly larger, shaped like a little stove, with the bottom floor given over in its entirety to a large receiving room. It did not come to a peak at the top, and was certainly less of a house because of it, as it lacked the far-reaching view that Vera had from her window.

"It's extremely appropriate," said Vera's mother, "that he has a house with no perspective on its surroundings."

On Sobek, it was customary to festoon all of the diplomatic residences with vibrant banners, painted by hand and depicting the flora and fauna of the visiting and host planets. They fluttered around these houses when the wind picked up at night, and were an ongoing reminder of the intended good will between the planets. These banners were the only way to distinguish the diplomatic buildings from those around them; they seemed prepared for a perpetual birthday party, one where there were sure to be extremely good favors.

Most ambassadors stationed on Sobek took pride in the creation of these banners, employing artists to paint them, and having them redone every few years when they began to look shabby, but the Earth ambassador was very lax, and the banners around his residence had faded quite a bit in the hot sun. It was rumored that he hadn't even commissioned new ones upon his arrival, and that the ones hanging had been done at the behest of his predecessor. For an example of a proper diplomatic residence, it was only necessary to go up the road to the house of the Slompernaut ambassador, who kept a fresh and tidy establishment, and always had teams of painters on his lawn at work on new banners.

The garden in which the Mironov's house stood was more than two acres, most of which lay between the ambassador's house and their own. The pathways between the houses were colonnaded by shade trees—among them species similar to trees that can be found on Earth—and their presence pointed to the extreme diligence of unnamed gardeners. It took some tending to develop them to the size they were in that inhospitable climate.

Though the garden was walled and the gate was closed, the custom on the planet was that the gardens belonged to everyone, and the law agreed. They were not owned at all, and the "deeds" to them were signed in ceremonial agreements by the sun and the sky. Any stranger in the world had the right to open the gate and go inside to take a nap beneath a flower bush in the heat of the day. This meant that it was common to find a visitor camping just beside the fountain when one looked outside the window in the morning. Whatever a human might say—and it is plain that a human would say a great deal—a Sobeki would simply raise her hand to say hello, and then go about her business, or if the owner of the house liked the looks of the person and wanted to chat, she might bring out a tray of coffee and cookies, and stay awhile to talk to the visitor. This was true whether the individual was a neighbor from town or a somewhat ragged stranger whom one did not know.

Vera was human through and through, however, and the very idea of a dirty stranger appearing out of nowhere and

*The cots on which the hobos sleep are standard-issue and available in most well-run town squares. They are kept in little huts to which the Custodian of the Square has a key. Also available are clean bedding and toothpick packets that look like lockpick sets. Sobekis always clean their teeth before bed most elaborately with a range of toothpicks.*

planting him or herself in the garden made her nervous beyond all measure. As yet, she had not ventured outside, and spent her time at the window of her room.

After that initial wave of excitement, the visit from the mayor and his staff, unpacking and putting together the furniture, exploring the garden with her parents and Alfonse, and taking pictures to send to her friends and family back on Earth, there was an inevitable lull. At a certain point, one has settled in and must actually begin to live in a place. Vera did not do this easily.

On one side of Vera's new house, just beyond the wall, was the vast quiet of the desert. On the other side was the street, busy with commuters during the day. From that side came the bells of the trams and the hoots of the footslogs, and the loud talk of people passing by and catching up with their neighbors on their way to and from work. Merchants came by selling fruit. At times they stopped their carts on the walkway in front of Vera's house, and a queue would form. Sobekis lingered there on the sidewalk, ate their fruit, rinsed their snouts in the fountain, and then went back about their business.

From the top window, Vera watched all this. Under their arms, the Sobekis on their way to work carried long skinny briefcases that looked particularly like baguettes, down to the knobbish ends. They swung these cases around as they walked, but folded them to their chests when they entered crowded trams so as not to hit each other.

Vera sat in this same position at the window and ate dry crackers—though she didn't like them—until the crackers were gone, even the crumbs.

Once, a passing worker caught sight of her leaning out

*These small eggs have a mild and pleasant taste, but the effort it takes to shell them is not worth it at all.*

the window and waved cheerfully. Vera was surprised—she had thought herself invisible in this top window—and returned a tentative wave. As soon as he had passed, she went back inside.

At breakfast, she was even quite rude to her mother, and sulked openly because there was no oatmeal.

"Now, Verochka, this looks exactly like oatmeal," said her mother, tasting the porridge with a wooden spoon. Normally her mother would have let her temper rise, but she was trying not to because of the circumstances.

"It's nothing like it!" barked Vera in outrage. Her mother scowled, but turned her back and ignored the outburst. Vera, who was actually hungry, got up and ladled out a bowl.

"I suppose it's fine," said Vera after a bite or two. Her mother continued to ignore her. Vera did not actually like to upset her mother when she could avoid it, and the cereal did taste fine. It wasn't much like oatmeal, but it was sweet and grainy, a little like millet. Vera's mother continued with the dishes and even began to whistle.

"How do the eggs taste?" Vera asked. You may note that

she did not actually apologize, but Vera's mother knew that she was trying to without actually saying it, and she came and sat down at the table.

"Very small," her mother replied.

Back on Earth, Vera's mother often had eggs and toast for breakfast, and today she had before her eggs and toast as well. The eggs were comically small, however, and the dish looked like it was filled with light-blue jellybeans. Resting on top was a hunk of incompressible bread that Vera's mother had poked at, unsuccessfully, with fire.

"Alfonse stocked the larder," Vera's mother said, eyeing the peculiar hillock in the bowl before her. "He was on his own recognizance, so I can't complain." She pushed away the eggs and began to gnaw on the hunk of bread at the side of her mouth. "The taste is quite nice," she said, moistening it cautiously.

Vera's father came in from the garden where he had been taking an early morning constitutional. He gestured toward the ambassador's house. "He's not hiding, you know. He's right over there. He's in the clearing doing some sort of peculiar calisthenics."

"Did you say hello?" Vera's mother asked.

"No," he replied. "Any preserves?"

She pointed to a little earthenware pot on the table.

"What fruit is it?"

"It tastes like haw," said Vera's mother. It is common knowledge that when you first arrive on a new planet, all the fruits taste like haw, though perhaps it is more an issue of one's sense of taste adapting to a new environment than of the food itself. Vera's mother ate a spoonful of jam thoughtfully, having given up on her original breakfast.

*The ambassador after calisthenics. The expression on his face is his standard one.*

None of them had yet talked to the ambassador, and he'd made no overtures, though they had just traveled two thousand light-years from his own home planet.

On several occasions, Vera had seen him from her window at the top of the house. He was a very old man, and clearly very irritable, for he never had a pleasant expression on his face, even when alone. He took a nap in the shade of a large boulevard tree every afternoon, in a spot behind a concealing boulder where it was clear he did not expect to be disturbed, even with the Sobeki policy about open gardens. Once or twice she had seen him crouch down and hide behind that boulder when he heard the squeak of the gate opening. Both times he had remained in the crouch until the visitors had left.

The ambassador's only charm was that he snored quite loudly, and drew a moving canopy of bugs around his head with the noise. He shielded his face with a yellow handkerchief while he slept, which made the whole thing even more amusing to Vera.

According to Alfonse, who arrived just then with a basket of groceries and the morning papers, the ambassador had not endeared himself generally in all his time on Sobek. "The ambassador's last aide stole his whisker trimmer and ran off into the night, you know."

"What did a Sobeki need with a whisker trimmer?" asked Vera's father.

"It was just for spite, as you might imagine. It took the ambassador two months to get a new one from Earth. We have nothing to trim here, and don't manufacture them.

"It is unfortunate that his wife is away again. She is buying pottery. I gather that she is trying to mount an exhibition

*Some recent purchases from Mary Cardshaw's collection. Sobekis are rightfully vain about their skin patterns, and some even commission pots based on their own or those of loved ones.*

on Earth." Alfonse lowered his eyes. "She is his only saving grace," he said, using an extremely discreet hand signal.

The ambassador was scheduled to deliver a very important speech in a week, to be shown on Sobeki television. This was not half as important as it would have been on Earth, however. Very few Sobekis owned televisions, and those that did used them primarily to watch concerts. Nevertheless, this speech held some importance for Vera's parents, it being their first assignment. The draft that Alfonse had brought over for them to work on was very poorly written, and was keeping them in an ongoing state of exasperation. Though they had not yet met him in person, their opinion of the ambassador was already tinted with animosity.

"It must take some effort to remain so ignorant," said Vera's mother.

"Or he is very stupid," suggested Alfonse with his ring finger flipped up in gesture and then quickly hidden.

Alfonse picked up the piece of bread that lay abandoned beside the breakfast plates and knocked it several times upon the table. "I suppose you didn't follow my instructions," he said with some amusement. "It's hardly edible like this!"

The conversation was conducted at such a rate that Vera could not possibly keep up. She found her mind drifting untethered, as it had so often recently. Vera thought of that great desert on the other side of that wall, and the wild animals who lived there. She had looked at many photographs back home on Earth, and had seen their fierce and awful visages. She had read, too, that at times the Wild Cutlers made it onto the cobbled streets of Drift City, and had to be netted by teams of Sobekis on footslogs, who trained a great deal for that eventuality.

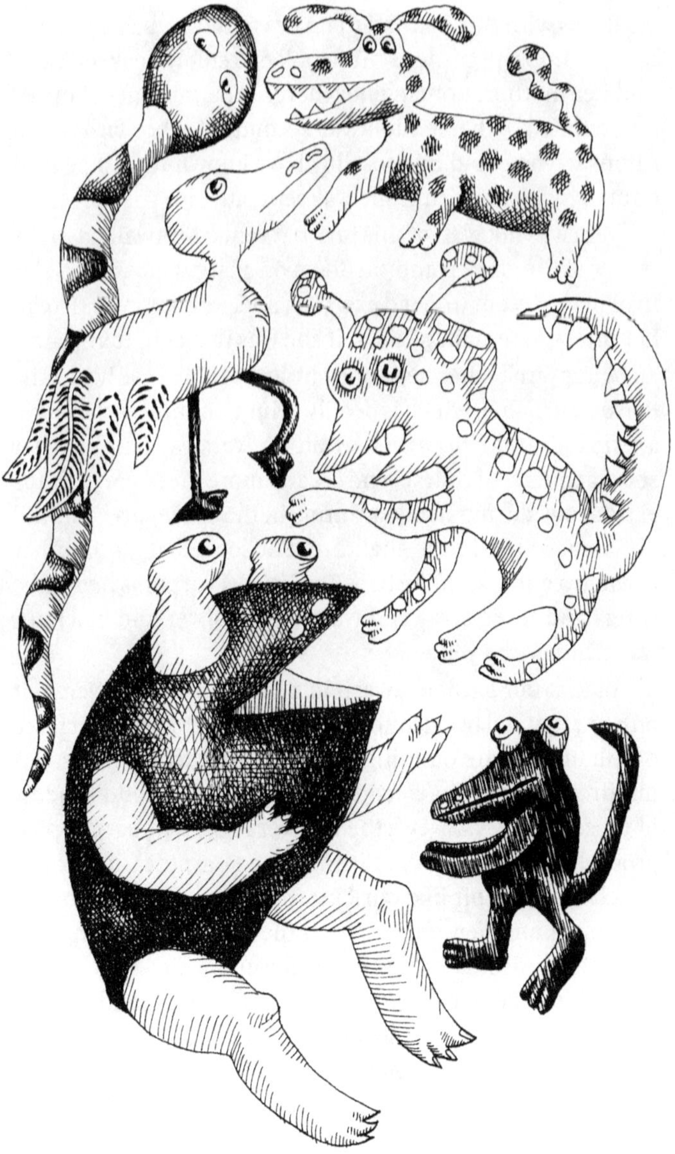

It was with this in mind that Vera found herself suddenly cast out into the garden. "You look extremely peaked, Vera," said her mother, noticing her there. "You must get some exercise today." The opinion was seconded by her father and Alfonse, who could not possibly have known what a peaked human looked like, and she was sent outside.

Vera was not glad of this turn of events. She walked to the center of the garden and sat down on a large, mossy boulder, firm in her intent to avoid exercise, and perhaps even firm in her intent to remain peaked, if she was in fact in that state.

A bug circled her head and she jumped, in case it was the Poison Turpulus, which is deadly to humans unless they have a series of shots before they are bitten. Vera had had all of her shots at home, of course, and several more that were perhaps extraneous during her quarantine in the spaceport. This did not assuage her in the slightest. She looked all around her to catch a glimpse of the bug. The Poison Turpulus had three wings and three eyes, and was colored silver and black, or was it green and yellow?

In that fair garden, awash in a luxury of shade, Vera felt only anxiety and peevishness. To be peevish took a great force of will in such surroundings, as Sobeki gardeners had spent hundreds of years in consideration of the light and shadow of these walkways. Nevertheless, Vera ignored that dappled ground. She ignored the flitting of the Karnoff's Brodrians, which looked a bit like our butterflies and trailed colors in the air around her. She ignored the fountain burbling gently, and the aroma of the sugar flowers, which was known to catch on the wind and carry long distances, and was immortalized most famously by an anonymous traveler to the old city: "Old lovers, though parted, pique to the scent of the sugar flower, for whom distance is nothing! Just so can love take great strides across the world on such a fragile breeze."

Then a fly bit her. Vera sat motionless. Twenty seconds was all it took for the Poison Turpulus to dispatch its prey. She rose, controlling herself as best she could. There was no time to run back to her parents if the vaccine somehow failed. She would walk calmly back to the house and tell them what had happened and hope that she did not drop onto the path before she made it to the steps. Though her heart was pounding noisily, she was still alive at the count of twenty.

Just as Vera finished her count and caught her breath, the ambassador appeared in front of her, heading in the other direction with his eyes down. He did not see what was before him. He was dressed in swimming trunks, and he had a pale green towel over his shoulder. When he finally saw her, he let out a yelp.

"A little woman!" he screeched, clutching the hairs on his thin, naked chest. Then he got ahold of himself. "No privacy on this path at all. The hobos are bad enough. A man can't bathe without scores of them, and now you must kick aside the shrimp as well."

"I'm the daughter of the new translators," said Vera, who was embarrassed by the behavior of the ambassador, and felt she should explain herself. "We just came from Earth."

"Did your parents bring me my things?" he asked quickly. "Did Alfonse retrieve them? I've heard nothing at all about it from him. I wouldn't be surprised in the slightest if he has shredded through the boxes with his wretched claws, and then hidden them from me."

Vera was silent. Alfonse kept his claws very nicely, she had noticed, and even if he did not, anyone could tell that

the ambassador's comment was unacceptably rude.

"Tell them to drop the boxes off outside my door as soon as they can," he said curtly, and edged her out of his way with a sharp "Pardon!"

Vera stood in the path for a moment, and then hid behind a nearby tree in case he came back. She stood there for several minutes, and then became further embarrassed by her own behavior, and walked quickly away from the tree and home without looking back.

Alfonse was still sitting at the kitchen table with her parents when Vera arrived back home.

"I met the ambassador on the path," Vera announced.

Alfonse clutched his heart in sympathy, and then signed discreetly under his armpit something that Vera's mother refused to translate.

"And I was bitten by a fly," Vera added.

"What did he say?" asked Vera's mother, who was unconcerned about the fly.

"He asked about some packages, and he was very rude about it, a complete besstydnik."

"He must have been on the way to one of his extremely long baths," Alfonse said. "He is maniacal about them, and is always irritable until he washes. You must not talk to him until then. He uses a deserted fountain on the far side of town because he doesn't like to take sociable baths." Alfonse tsked. Sobekis liked to congregate in big groups, and share gossip, laugh and horse around while they bathed. Entire extended family groups would make dates, and meet at such and such an hour and such and such a fountain. "Oh no," he continued, "he must bathe his tail in the secrecy of night." And he shook his head again.

This, Vera's mother explained later, was a folk expression. "Oh, it means something about sneakiness, or perhaps perversion. Your father and I haven't quite worked out the nuance on that one yet."

## X

As unwilling as she had been to leave the house and her parents' side before, after her encounter with the ambassador and the traumatic fly bite (which, by the way, had not even required a dollop of salve), Vera was doubly so.

Her parents were very busy with work, however, and even had frequent meetings to attend in the evenings. Try as Vera might to convince them, she was not allowed to go along, and Alfonse was left behind in charge.

It was good to have company, but he spoke barely a word of Russian, and mainly sat at the table reading the paper, nibbling on wheaten biscuits, and listening to tinny music on the portable radio he carried along for these visits. Periodically he looked up and smiled. "Khorosho?" he would ask with a tentative thumbs-up, and then when she said it was, he would put his head back down to his reading.

On these evenings, Vera remembered with great fondness the college student who used to watch her in Moscow. Masha would bring along her manicure kit and paint Vera's nails, affixing stars to the tips quite professionally. Masha was in her second year at the Polytechnic, studying to be an engineer, but she always had time to learn the new dance moves and teach them to Vera.

Clearly, Alfonse was not a babysitter like that, and between the two of them it was extremely awkward. Vera went to her room while he was over, as much to be polite to him as anything, for it certainly caused him a strain when he tried to communicate unsuccessfully.

When Vera's parents were home it was hardly better, as they were utterly distracted. Occasionally her mother would stop what she was doing and frown, and look over at Vera thoughtfully. "It's too bad we've arrived during a holiday. I'm sure we'll all be relieved when you start school."

Vera did not agree with that, for the prospect of school churned her stomach as well, and she said nothing in reply.

"Please, Verochka. Go outside," her mother said. "The lock to the front door will open again in one hour. Unless you have an injury, you may not come back into the house for that amount of time."

Vera scowled, but got up and went out. She could not refuse her mother, especially when she knew her parents had so much work to do. Moreover, though she seemed unable to leave the house, she was very, very tired of it.

Vera was only several paces from the house, with one foot on the garden path, when she saw someone walking toward her. It was a Sobeki, certainly not full size, perhaps about Vera's age, it was not easy for her to tell. Vera stood stock-still and watched her approach. Though she knew that it was rude to stop and stare at someone as they approached, Vera could not help it, and did not even try to.

The Sobeki was dressed, which was strange in and of itself. Stranger still, she wore not only an accessory here or there, as Sobekis sometimes did, but a full outfit in the manner that it would be worn on Earth, with the torso completely covered. In fact, she was dressed exactly as a child might be when going out to play in the park on Earth. She had on a t-shirt, a pair of shorts, and red-laced sneakers in the style of Earth shoes, though quite a bit bigger. She appeared also to

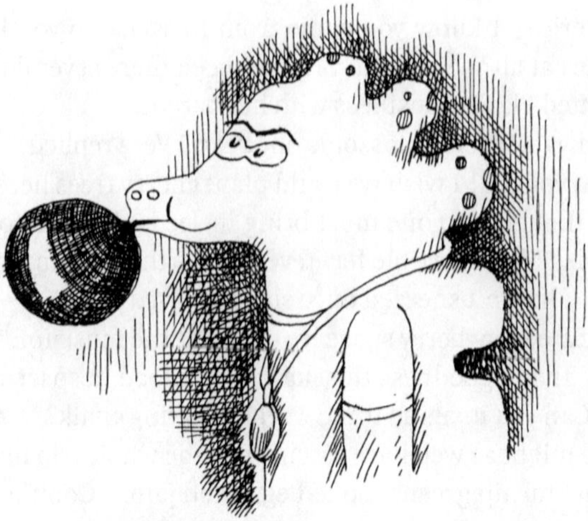

*Connie Blanche Qui-deeé*

be chewing bubble gum. Vera wondered for a moment how the mayor would respond to all the "Earth-style" clothing the girl wore after his talk about the vacationers and their shoes. This went far beyond those fashionable water shoes that had introduced the shrimp into the city.

"Are you Vera Yevgenyevna?" She used Vera's Earth name very politely, just as Vera's own mother had coached her to do when talking to Sobekis. This too was surprising, and Vera looked closely at her in amazement, for she had not yet met a Sobeki who could pronounce her name. The Sobeki spoke perfectly. She even seemed to have an Earth accent, maybe American. Vera nodded nervously in response.

"My name is Connie Blanche Qui-deeé. I was born on Earth, you know, which is why my name is Connie Blanche, and I lived there for my first seven years, in Washington, DC, in America. I know you come from Russia. Do you know America at all?" Vera did. She had been there several times on United Planets business with her parents.

"I saw the cherry blossoms one year," Vera replied.

"Oh, you did! I wish we could plant cherry trees here. We can't, though. No one must bring in seeds; it's bad for the animals. I have terrible hay fever on Earth, but I'm fine on Sobek. I haven't sneezed once since I moved here."

"We ate strawberry space ice cream at the museum," said Vera. "Thank goodness they have better food in space nowadays. Can you imagine three weeks of eating chalk?"

"We might as well have eaten chalk the whole trip here. It was just turnip greens, boiled eggs and jam." Connie shuddered. "Not much of a kitchen."

"Not really?!" said Vera, but Connie didn't reply to that.

"My parents are translators like yours," she said. "They told me all about you, and I read about you in the paper before you came. Did you see the article?"

Vera hadn't.

"Oh, I'll bring it over for you. You can scrapbook it."

Vera agreed that she would like a copy. Connie's mention of the newspaper made her think of how she had planned to send home dispatches to her classmates at the Strugatsky School. She hadn't yet made a move to do it, but it was true that they might enjoy having a copy of a Sobeki newspaper to put up on the corkboard.

"I would have visited sooner, but I was sick for a week. Really flat on my back. My tail was as cold as ice! It was the mayor who gave me your address. He thought we might be able to hang up his signs. The children are away for the Broomstick Holiday, mostly. Do you know about his work on the shrimp?" Vera nodded, and Connie suddenly grabbed her arm and blurted out, "I couldn't wait to meet you, Vera. I am so lonely for Earth!"

This was the happiest thing Vera had heard in ages.

"Lonely for Earth!" said Vera. "I can't stand it! I would run off and stow away on a ship to get back home if I knew it wouldn't hurt my parents' feelings."

Connie outstretched her hand, and Vera shook it enthusiastically. It would be clear to an outside observer that both girls had spent a good deal of time around adults, for they grasped each others' elbows after the fashion commonly seen in the halls of the Jyptodome.

"Do your parents work for the embassy, too?" Vera asked.

"They used to, but they quit to write their memoirs. The people here are very interested in Earth and want to hear all about it. There's big money in it, and my parents don't really like to work. They are against it on principle, in fact. They are hoping to make a lot this way so they can retire, and spend their time lounging in the garden. Who can blame them? I don't want to work when I'm older; it seems boring."

Vera laughed at that. "You are supposed to find a job that you like, if you can. That's why you go to school."

Connie nodded. "I know. I've heard that frequently, but my parents are bohemians. They told me I don't have to go to school if I don't want to."

Vera was impressed. "I'm supposed to go to school," she told Connie, "and I'm supposed to study hard and get good grades. My parents have been very clear about that."

"Well, I do go to school now. I like it, actually. School is very good here, I have to admit. It's much better than on Earth," Connie said. "Though it's the only thing," she added

*After much training at grown-up events, both girls are quite adept at polite greetings.*

quickly. She did not like to seem disloyal to her first world. "You know, they even have Earth restaurants here. That's how much the Sobekis like Earth."

Vera laughed. "But Earth is a whole planet. We have a million different kinds of food there! What could they possibly serve?"

"They have a strange assortment of foods from all over the world. It's whatever recipes they can pick up in their travels, and it never makes sense at all. I've heard, though, that someone else has hired a consultant, and will be opening an Austrian café. That will be very nice. I think we could be consultants, too, if we ever wanted to go into business! They'll take anybody who knows anything, even children.

"If you are homesick sometimes, you can go. I'll take you. When I first came, I used to go there and eat corn flakes every morning. Finally, my mother said it was too expensive, and looked into ordering me a crate from Earth. Do you know, the crate would have cost ten thousand krucks?"

Vera whistled, although she really had no idea about the exchange rate.

"Yes, but I like them very much. I ate them every morning for the first seven years of my life."

"You didn't eat them when you were a baby, though, did you?" said Vera, who could be a bit of a stickler, like both of her parents.

"Yes," said Connie stoutly, "even then. They ground it up in a baby-food mill."

Vera did not have an answer to that. "I'd like to see an Earth restaurant," she said instead.

"I'll take you when I have a little money. Right now I'm too broke for that. I warn you, it's really not that close to what you know. They tried to decorate it like Earth, but you'll see what they came up with."

"I miss home!" Vera burst out, and was glad to admit it, as she couldn't just say it outright to her parents. She felt tears springing up, though normally she would have been ashamed to cry in front of a stranger.

"Of course you do! I was sick for the first year. Actually sick. I had to go to a doctor because I was getting headaches and having trouble sleeping. But then I felt better, no thanks to the doctor, though she tried. What can they do if you have a problem with your feelings? I'm sure it won't take you that long. My father says I can be very sensitive. He's the worst of them all. He takes to his bed sometimes, you know."

"And what does your mother do?" asked Vera.

"We order dinner from a restaurant."

Connie continued. "On Earth, my mother baked cookies when people felt bad, though then she would criticize them if they ate too many. My mother has been telling me since we moved that Earth baking soda doesn't work on Sobek. I think she just doesn't want us to eat cookies any longer. She thinks my teeth have come in soft like human teeth."

"I don't think our teeth are so bad. We can chew steak and all that," said Vera.

Connie shrugged. "That's just what my mom says, not me. She's not really as open-minded as I am, even though she lived on Earth for so long. The older generation can be peculiar."

Vera considered whether her parents were open-minded. Perhaps, she admitted to herself, she was even less so than they were.

"Would you like to go around town and hang up posters

with me?" Connie asked. "I figure if we take the afternoon, we could see the sights, and I can introduce you to some people. At the end, we'd have a little money to buy some candy."

"That sounds very nice," said Vera, who was surprised to think so. She had thought there could be no worse idea in the world when she'd heard about the posters from the mayor. "But I'll have to ask my mother."

Connie went along with Vera to her house. The door was locked, as promised, and Vera knocked on the window.

"You have ten more minutes, Vera, and you can just sit out there on the steps. I will not let you inside a minute earlier," said her mother through the door.

"No, no, Mama. I met a girl, and she and I are going to put up posters for the mayor. She's from Earth!"

Vera's mother popped out the door.

"My name is Connie Blanche Qui-deeé. I'm from Washington, DC, originally, but we moved here a year and a half ago so my parents could write their memoirs. My parents are translators, too. Do you know them?"

"Oh, hello. How lovely to meet you! I believe we did meet your parents on Earth. Your mother is Bluet, and your father is Bertrand?"

Connie nodded.

Vera's father poked his head out. "We were seated next to them at a dinner once in the United Planets dining room. I seem to remember a very bland tofu patty and asparagus. Your father and I talked about ping pong, which he had just taken up, and we made plans to play, though somehow it never happened."

"He's still crazy about it!" said Connie. "He's gotten half the neighborhood to play with him. He's got club patches,

*Although on Earth, enthusiasts insist on calling the game "table tennis," on Sobek "ping pong" is the preferred name for it, since the name sounds similar to a Sobeki phrase meaning "very clever."*

and even the mayor likes to come out for a game. But everyone knows the mayor will go anywhere, and always hangs around. Sometimes you have to kick him out, he stays so long."

"Tell your parents we said hello," said Vera's father.

"And we'd love to have them to dinner as soon as we're settled," added Vera's mother. Then they both turned back anxiously to the speech lying before them on the table.

As it stood on the page, the ambassador had gone out of his way to insult local customs, the education system, and the local hospitals in his speech for television. "If we translate this word as 'fellowship' instead of 'discord,' that would change the whole sense of the paragraph for the better, . . ." Vera's father was saying to her mother as the two girls left the house.

*A traditional Sobeki cart might be decorated by its owner with any number of Sobeki symbols and images from nature. Occasionally, when a Sobeki is mad enough, the carts are painted with testimonies to his or her personal grudges.*

# XI

CONNIE and Vera rolled the cart filled with the mayor's posters down the sandy street. The walk was paved with what Earth people might consider an impractical mix of small, bright stones and shells that broke any mechanical device that hadn't been designed and built on Sobek, but the Sobekis considered first that it glittered prettily, and made any subsequent decisions based on that. On Sobek, one did not replace something beautiful with something merely utilitarian.

They pushed their cart through the center of town. The mayor had specified that the signs should only go up in shops and on busy streets. "Don't put them on back roads or places where no one congregates. You might even put them in one or two of the more popular gardens, if you can. The Pee-A-Wees on Trandor Street get a lot of traffic, especially by those outstanding bushes overhanging the gate."

The mayor had supplied Connie with wooden poles on which to attach the signs, and though the poles had a sharpened end, it was quite an affair to knock them into the dirt so that they could be freestanding. Both girls had to grab hold of the post, and on the count of three, shove it down as hard as they could. The mayor, foreseeing the difficulty, had supplied thick work gloves, clearly Earth-made, for Vera to use. Of course, Connie didn't need them.

"Jackie Schubert left them behind," read the note that was stuffed inside. "Be certain to return them to me, for reasons of sentiment."

The sign painter responsible for the posters had taken a great deal of artistic care over the problem of the shrimp. The signs were hand-printed on sheets of silk, though the funny shrimp in the middle was surrounded with harsh words that didn't match the fluttering material it was on, pale blue to sooth the eye.

Connie translated the sign for Vera: "Stop, friends! Your negligence and selfish, style-obsessed habits have led to an invasion of bile fish. That may be fine for you, but the mayor's office wants them out! Stop wearing shoes in the fountains, and collect any shrimp you see for return to the mayor's office. Toner fifty per shrimp is the bounty—though you hardly deserve a reward for a problem you yourself caused!"

Vera laughed. "That's hardly the way to win over supporters!"

"I don't suppose he cares, but it isn't how they do it at UP meetings." The two girls laughed together as they considered the kind of polite and roundabout ways everything was stated at the UP. "Good friends, neighbors, I wouldn't say it if I didn't absolutely have to, but I've noticed some extra shrimp have appeared here and there," might have been one UP approach.

Vera and Connie put several signs at intervals in dirt pits on the main thoroughfare, and both girls found themselves covered in dirt that had kicked up. Vera was pouring sweat. The sun was high, and she considered that early morning might have been a more appropriate time for the job. Connie did not seem to notice the heat especially, and Vera could not see that she perspired at all. But Connie had lived on Earth long enough to know the vulnerabilities of humans, and Vera was surprised she hadn't considered it.

"My goodness," said Vera, "you don't have a canteen in there, do you?"

Connie did not. "There's a spigot," she pointed.

"That's lucky," said Vera, as they cupped their hands, and both drank their fill. The water was delicious and very cold.

"No, not at all," said Connie. "There is a spigot on every block." After quenching their thirst and running cold water over the tops of their heads, they went back to their work.

"This is labor," said Connie. "I wonder if the mayor is even aware that there are laws about this on other worlds."

"Do children work here?" Vera asked.

"Only at the jobs they like to do," Connie replied.

They hung a sign on a prominent wall with their bucket of paste and a brush. This drew several mothers who were pushing their babies in carriages. They stopped to discuss the sign quietly.

Next, Vera and Connie came to a small flower shop. In the front window, they could see a young florist intertwining flowering vines with blooms to make a wreath. Sobekis have larger fingers than humans, but they are extremely nimble. The florist was intent upon a large platter stacked high with flowers that had been grouped by color. He took a minute and hummed thoughtfully before reaching for the next one.

"They like flowers very much here," Connie said to Vera. Vera supposed that most people did, and did not chalk this up to any individuality in the Sobekis. "No, it is a particular trait," said Connie, "just as on Earth we are very sneaky."

Vera would have replied angrily, but Connie had included herself in it. Were Earth people particularly sneaky? Vera didn't think so. But were they viewed as such by people on other planets? Vera would have to ask her parents. The peo-

*Just like on Earth, mothers and fathers on Sobek transport their small children in strollers. Unlike on Earth, you will also see mothers and fathers on Sobek pushing their unhatched eggs in little strollers made just for the purpose. They sew cosies for their eggs with a little hole on top called a "breather," though of course the eggs don't really need air holes for breathing.*

ple from Earth that she knew were almost exclusively frank and trustworthy.

"Hello," said Connie as they entered the shop. "Beautiful wreaths! We're working on a public safety program. Do you mind if we put up a poster?" The florist smiled at them, and took the sign to read. After a moment he looked up and waggled a flower at them, and began to speak very rapidly and with evident irritation.

"What does he say?" asked Vera, who was not entirely pleased to be lectured by an adult, whether or not she understood the content. This was a thing she generally did her best to avoid.

"Well, he doesn't think the mayor should be asking children to do his dirty work," Connie said as the man paused his tirade to let her translate. "This whole anti-shoe business is a dirty thing, he says. He enjoys wearing shoes in the water for their own sake, not for fashion at all. They become quite squishy and waterlogged, and he likes the sensation."

Again the florist paused, and now it seemed that the wind had gone out of his sails a little, for he talked in a calmer voice. "It makes him irate that the mayor should define what sort of sensations we ought to pursue."

The florist smiled and pointed at Connie's feet. "He also feels that since I clearly like to wear shoes myself, I am a turncoat to the cause of personal expression." Connie translated the last bit to Vera proudly; she was flattered to be attacked personally as it meant the florist considered her an adult of some sort. She replied to the man with great cheer, and then translated her own words to Vera. "I said that the issue is the shrimp, not the shoes. Does he want to have shrimp all over him when he's bathing?"

Connie paused and waited for a reply. "He supposes not."

The florist made one more resigned comment, and finally gestured to his front window. They hung the sign.

He seemed to feel apologetic as well. Most people, all but the most ornery, feel terrible after yelling at children, and he handed them each a flower on their way out. In an extremely strained Russian he added, "Very nice meeting you, Earth girl."

Vera mustered what she hoped was Sobeki for "Very nice to meet you, too." The florist chuckled and went back to his work.

Stepping onto the street, Vera put her flower behind her ear, and Connie tucked hers into the top of her shirt.

"Sometimes I wish I had an ear," said Connie wistfully, "but I don't suppose you can hear as well as we do."

"Of course we can hear as well!" said Vera.

"How would you know if you did?" asked Connie. "You would have to know what I hear."

"And vice versa," said Vera.

"On Earth, I felt sure my friends couldn't hear as well. For instance, they were never much for identifying birds."

"That's not a matter of hearing, is it?" Vera said sternly. "That's knowledge and memory."

"Maybe so," said Connie, "but I say it's because you can't hear all the notes they sing."

They walked down the street to the next store. "I'll translate for you until you learn the language," said Connie, "but you have to dive in, you know, or you won't ever. By tomorrow you have to really try to talk to people, even if they don't have the foggiest clue what you're saying."

Vera had already noticed a very bossy streak in Connie.

Still, it was comforting in a way, since a bossy streak wasn't at all strange or alien.

"How are you at learning languages?" Connie asked.

Vera whistled the sound that meant "okay" in Sobeki.

"Well that sounded like it, at least. I tried to teach my friend Mary some basic stuff, but she really couldn't get anywhere. They say you have thick tongues, and that makes it hard for you to get out some of our sounds. I don't think it's true, though. I think the trouble is really with your ears. Your languages are no trouble for *us* to pronounce, even with the difference in *our* tongues."

Vera scoffed, a little offended. She didn't reply what she felt, which was: "At least we don't have plain, old nostril holes in the sides of our heads." She simply said, "Humph," and called it a victory for her own self-control.

Connie heard the angry humph. "You can't be hurt anytime people point out a difference, Vera dear."

Vera held her tongue, though it was doubly insulting both to be insulted, and to be criticized for having been insulted.

"I was the only Sobeki at my school in DC," Connie went on, "but I didn't care about that. First of all, there were all types of other children there, not just human, but secondly, I know we are a beautiful species, and no one can tell me otherwise. I hope you don't have very poor self-esteem, Vera, or you will be extremely unhappy here."

This too bothered Vera. "I like myself fine. I think humans are very beautiful, too."

"When I started school, I was very self-conscious. Then I began going around with this Chalcian girl named Willie who was extremely headstrong. My mother says I turned into a bit of a chauvinist after that."

"I thought you loved Earth above everything."

"Oh, I do," said Connie, "but it's important to love yourself, too."

"Well, you don't show that by talking against other people's ears," said Vera. "That might be considered very rude by some." They were silent for a bit after that, pushing the cart in tandem. Connie did seem to go too far, Vera thought. It was no wonder her parents no longer worked for the UP. If they were halfway as opinionated and bossy as their daughter, Vera imagined they would botch up all negotiations. Vera laughed a little at that thought. Her own parents sometimes had a hard time reining in their opinions, as well.

They went on to a paper goods store down the block. It sold lovely pens and stationery, and stamps carved from tiny chunks of quartz. The stationer, who was sorting boxes at the back when they entered, waved warmly at them, and came up to shake Vera's hand.

"You are the Earth girl, of course. How was your trip? We are delighted to have you."

"I am delighted to be here," said Vera sincerely. "Everyone I've met has been very welcoming."

"They may have been," the stationer said, "but of course you must not fall in with a bad element." She beetled her brow significantly in the direction of the posters.

"Do you mean the shrimp?" asked Connie.

"Oh, no one in particular, though the mayor shouldn't be hounding anyone about what they wear. There is no citywide dress code, after all."

Connie shrugged.

"I don't like to be singled out for wearing shoes. However, it is a very nice sign. Really gets its point across."

The stationer was not so opposed to the cause as the florist had been, but she had a good deal positive to say about the shrimp, and did not agree that they were a nuisance. "There is something compelling in their faraway gaze," she said as she brought out a book of sketches that she had drawn at the fountain around the corner. "See how that long whisker stands expectantly?"

Looking at the sketches seemed to clarify her decision. Finally, the stationer said, "Well, I can't support this program as it is, but I do hope we can find a solution that works for the shrimp, too." She shook both of their hands and sent them on their way.

The bookseller was much more amenable to the mayor's position, as was the librarian at the Weet-weet-weet Street Library of Poetry on the corner. Both of them found the recent move toward shoes enraging, an erosion of propriety and common sense.

"You see," said the librarian, a tall, thin Sobeki with extremely pointed ridges, "I am not a traditionalist. I love the forward motion of history, change, progress and all of that. This is why I love and embrace our visitors from other worlds, like you, Vera, and I hope to see you in here frequently, borrowing books!

"Still, I hate those stupid shoes and those stupid fools who wear them all the time. And yes, I will admit it, I could use the bounty money. I'm saving up to buy a camper. I plan on taking a sabbatical and going across to Klampoxia!"

"Everyone seems very happy to have you here, Vera," said Connie cheerfully as they left the store.

Vera hadn't noticed it at first, but she was enjoying their walk through the city. She enjoyed hearing, through Connie,

*The stationer shows Vera and Connie a sketch of the bile fish on extremely good rag paper, which is also sold in the store.*

the opinions of the Sobekis on the street and in the shops, and she even imagined at times she understood the gist of their words. She saw in one or two of their faces, though their features were so different, the familiar expressions of people from home. Certainly they weren't fearsome when they were all around her. They seemed somewhat regular, in fact.

It was true that Connie was bossy and a little critical, and also a bit of a braggart—she had spent inordinate time telling Vera about her victories as captain of her softball team back on Earth—but she was quite funny, and told Vera amusing stories about everyone in town. "Those ladies—there in the shade drinking coffee—potted so many Calinbirds that they gave themselves allergies. They were forced to move out until a cleaning service could come. And that man over there planted a ton of seeds in his neighbor's garden, just out of spite, to throw off the color scheme, but it all worked out in the end. The strange colors have made it the most popular garden in the area."

"You should be glad you ended up here, Vera," said Connie. "Sobek is actually very nice. Before we moved back here we spent six months on Capious Delta. Do you know anything about it?"

Vera didn't.

"The inhabitants are your type of people, but very tall and skinny, with long arms. They make tremendous pickpockets on account of their reach. It's a big problem on the trains there."

"I'm used to crime," said Vera, glad to have an opportunity to seem more worldly and cavalier than her new friend. "I grew up in a big city." Her parents had taught her not to be rude, even if provoked, and she could only ever brag for one sentence before she felt bad about it and changed course. "It must have been hard for you to get around," she added.

"Yes! All the mothers are so overprotective there that kids our age have to be chaperoned wherever they go. Teenagers aren't allowed out together, even in big groups, except for the ones causing trouble, of course. Just like everywhere, those ones go wherever they like."

"That sounds terrible."

"It is! If you like it on Earth, you won't like it there. And if you like it here, you'd find it intolerable over there. My parents were working so hard that they could never take me anywhere, and I just sat in the house all day and cried."

Vera listened with great sympathy. "That sounds really lonely."

"It was. My parents bought me a little bird to keep me company, but then we had to leave it when we left the planet."

"That's even worse."

"I don't think the bird minded, though. I left it with an older lady who lived next door. You can't really bring pets from planet to planet. They like it less than we do."

"I had to leave my pets at home, too."

"Oh, it's terribly wrenching to leave Earth, isn't it? I miss it so much. It's not bad here, though. You'll see that you'll like it in the end."

Vera did not reply.

"I know you will. You must trust me. And Vera, I was terrible to remark on your ears. I promise not to say another word. I admit it, I am very jealous of them sometimes. It comes from so many years living among you. I didn't like to have to wear my sunglasses pince-nez when we went to Florida for vacation."

“That’s ridiculous,” said Vera. “It’s no better or worse to have ears than not.”

“My parents say the same thing, though it doesn’t help that much when you grow up admiring all the earrings and barrettes Earth children have. But I’m not sure I would really like ears, after all. They might get in the way. And we do have lovely patterning on our skin, don’t you think?”

“Of course,” said Vera, patting her new friend’s arm, and they went off down the road together, smiling.

*All juice available at the stand is hand-squeezed by the vendor and her children in a large tub behind their house. This explains the occasional presence of small leaves or flowers that were not part of the original recipe.*

## XII

ONLY half-done with their job and worn out from the hot sun, for even Connie was not immune to the rigors of hard work in the heat of the day, they came upon a juice stand in the shade at the side of the road, and Connie proposed that they stop.

"My mother gave me some change so I could treat you to a juice. She told me to tell you that humans must be careful not to get dehydrated on Sobek."

"Yes, my father told me, too."

"Well, that's good, but I suppose I must look after you until you can do it for yourself."

Vera smiled.

From amid the gentle flutter of the bunting that decorated her stand, the juice vendor peered out in alarm at the two girls, and said something urgently to Connie.

"She says: 'Under her hat she is looking alarmingly pink. Has she cooked, do you think?'"

"I haven't cooked," said Vera to the woman. "I'm just hot, and my face is flushed." Connie translated Vera's words, listened to the vendor's response, and said to Vera, "I'm so relieved! I don't know how we might reverse it, were she no longer raw."

Vera looked at the vendor and wondered if she was serious. It appeared that she was, so Vera replied, "Don't worry, I won't cook at these temperatures any more than you will."

The vendor looked embarrassed. She tinkled the ice in the pitcher nearest her to change the subject.

“Her son is a great fan of Earth,” said Connie to Vera. “He insists on being called by his Earth name, Ivan, and he has a pen pal in Cincinnati, Cynthia, whom he talks about all the time. I’ve even sent her a letter myself, once or twice. She has very nice freckles just about everywhere.”

The vendor chimed in at the mention of Cynthia’s freckles. “She says they’re a bit small, though, and don’t really draw the eye,” translated Connie.

“What do these flags mean?” Vera asked.

“Oh, they give information on the health attributes of the juices.”

“That’s just like on Earth. They advertise all the medicinal qualities for everything.”

“Yes, that’s true, although they can claim anything here. They assume you are not so gullible, and anyway, most folks find little half-truths to be terribly amusing. This one says, ‘Tickles your colon delightfully,’ and that one says, ‘Drink a glass a day to bring true love to your doorstep.’” Connie shrugged. “Juice is very important culturally. It is because it takes so much effort to cultivate the fruit.”

They ordered their juices, and the vendor began the process of concocting them, all the while remarking about how sorry Ivan would be when he found out that he had missed them.

Vera repeated several friendly things that she had learned from her tapes, specifically the unit entitled “Polite Greetings on Sobek,” and the vendor smiled in approval.

“Ochen priyatno,” she said, patting Vera’s hand where it lay on the counter. Then she leaned over and asked something eagerly that Vera had no chance of understanding.

Connie translated: “She wants to know what you pin your

hair onto. She can't keep hers from falling off."

With a firm finger to her lips, Vera stifled her laughter, though it threatened to burst from her as though a leak had been sprung; she did not want to embarrass the vendor any further. Vera lifted up her hair, showed the vendor her roots, and let her examine them up close, which the vendor, after procuring her reading glasses from the shelf below, did at great length.

Having satisfied the vendor's curiosity, Vera and Connie said their goodbyes and rolled their cart back down the street, much revived by the juice. Perhaps it did exhibit some of those advertised properties, for they were able to hang the rest of the posters without another break. As they finished their work, Vera hummed a little tune. She did not realize that it was the mayor's sunrise song, but it had caught in her mind somehow, and Connie, who knew the melody well, hummed along.

"Let's have a soak," said Connie. "The afternoon is a nice time to go. It won't be too crowded."

Vera thought a dip in cool water sounded good and said so, but from all she had heard, she thought it would be very strange. In her mind was an image of a crowd of Sobekis bobbing up and down, periodically taking sips of their bathwater.

"Is there a protocol to it?" Vera asked. "I don't want to be rude by accident."

"Oh, there's no protocol," said Connie, who always stood up taller when she was asked to explain something. "You just wade in and take a drink from the spigot, or you sit down or stand in the middle and talk to your neighbors. You can submerge in the shade of the center, and sometimes stay there for hours if the conversation is good. It's quite nice to pass a day that way."

When they got to the fountain there was a problem immediately evident. Rippling in waves, gamboling through the surf that they themselves had created by their motion, lounging on all surfaces flat or angled, and clustered especially in groups under the spigots, were the shrimp.

"It wasn't like this before I got sick," said Connie. "Only one or two. They're sort of charming in small numbers."

"My goodness!" exclaimed Vera as they moved in closer for a look. "They don't bite, do they? Do they have venomous skin or anything?" asked Vera, examining a particularly fulsome shrimp that sat on the rim. "Are they electric?"

"I don't think so. Wouldn't they have mentioned it on the posters?"

"Would they have?"

"Maybe they don't know." Connie shrugged. "I know they're not venomous for I've heard stories of folks who've cooked them, and nothing happened."

Vera wasn't reassured. "Perhaps they're not venomous to you, but that doesn't say anything about humans."

"I suppose," said Connie, thoughtfully. "But you know," she chided, "there have been humans on Sobek for years."

Vera was irritated to find that Connie's supercilious remark reassured her.

"We'll just have to clear space to get through, I guess," Connie said. "I don't think it's good practice to get stymied."

Vera unfortunately had to agree. She herself had always been the most adamant of her friends on that point.

They got in gingerly and, pushing away the shrimp as they waded, moved toward a spot where cool water rushed from a spout and the shrimp were not so thick.

"I see what the mayor was so upset about," said Vera.

Connie nodded.

"What's it like normally?" Vera asked. They stood stock-still, and even Connie could not make herself submerge in the rippling pink lake.

"Well," Connie said, and paused. "It's much better, usually. Still, we're cooler, aren't we?"

"Much cooler," said Vera stoically.

"Another time, when the shrimp have been rounded up, we'll come back," Connie said. They soaked for a moment, long enough only to claim that they had done so, and then waded quickly out of the fountain, at just the careful pace that ensured they would not fall into the mass of shrimp as they went.

"We'll do our part," said Connie. "We really have to help clean this up."

Vera agreed.

"We can spend the bounty right away. Should I go home for another bag?"

"No," said Vera, who was getting tired, and had noticed that the sun was low. "Let's just fill what we have." There were several canvas bags left over in the cart.

"They seem to have no survival skills at all," said Vera as she picked up a shrimp easily. "They're like the dodo."

Connie nodded.

"I wonder why they've had any difficulty moving them," said Vera.

"It seems that no one has really tried."

It was clear that everyone was staying as far away as possible from the situation. The fountain was now empty except

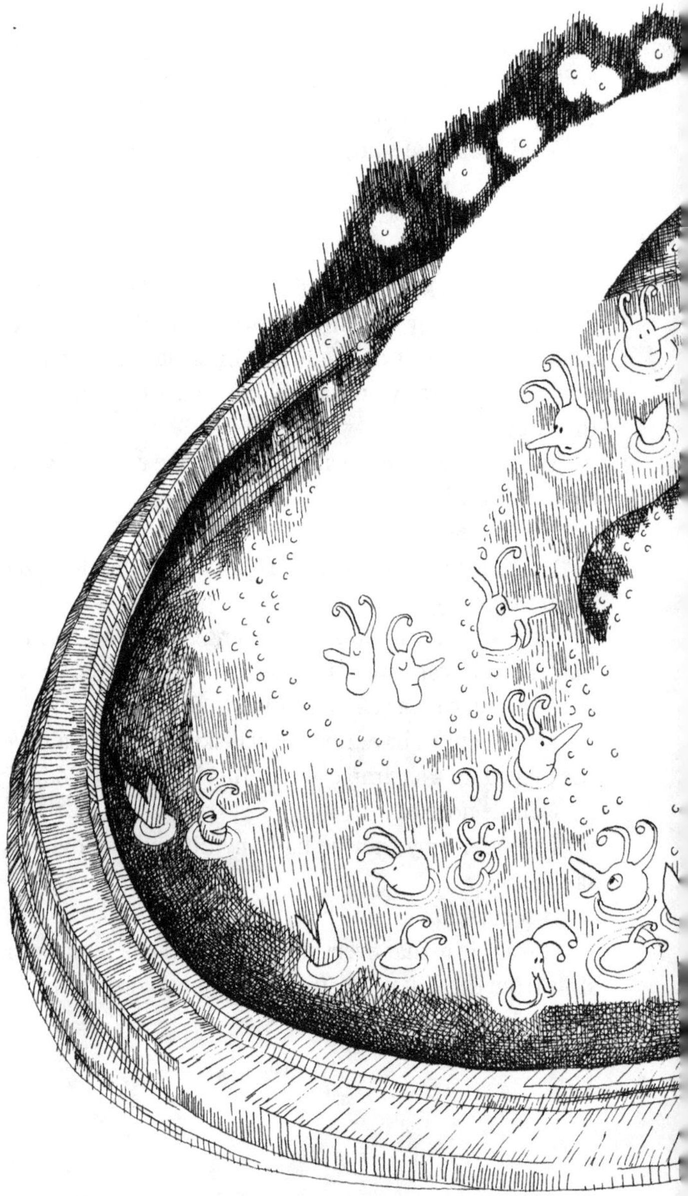

for the shrimp. The girls filled up their bags with little effort, but it made no dent in the shrimp population. The shrimp moved immediately into any space as soon as it was vacated.

"I suppose they'll need many volunteers to get a handle on this," Connie said, staring into the froth. "It's clearly too much work for the Custodian of the Square." She pointed at a gentleman sitting in the sunshine across from them. He was engaged in some sort of game with an older Sobeki in a hat, and considering his next move thoughfully. He put the stone counter down on the chosen spot and looked up to see the girls with their bags full of shrimp. He waved at them, and gave them a thumbs up for their efforts in collection. Connie held open her bag to show him how many she'd gotten.

"Good work, girls," he said cheerfully. "Keep it up and we'll get there in no time!" Then he went back to his game.

After gently stowing the bags of shrimp in the cart, the girls made their way to the mayor's office.

"They're quivering around in there," said Vera.

Connie stopped the cart to take a look, and poked one of the bags gingerly, watching it ripple as the shrimp rearranged themselves. She shrugged. "They seem fine to me."

At the front desk of the mayor's office, Barthes, the assistant whom Vera had met at her housewarming party, sat weaving a small basket out of reeds in several shades of green.

"Very nice craftsmanship," said Connie.

Barthes smiled. "Do you like it? I'm thinking of quitting the mayor's office and working full-time on this." He held it up to consider. "I'm imagining demand will go up now. Useful for shrimp collection, you know."

The girls agreed.

"Have you come for payment? That's thirty koblanks for

*Frankly, unlike a lifeguard at the seashore, the Custodian of the Square has little to do beyond sweeping up and managing keys. He or she can afford to nap frequently, and frequently does.*

the posters, and what was it? A half-lurling a shrimp?"

"Toner fifty," said Connie.

Barthes got the money out of a small lidded basket at his feet, clearly his handiwork, then dumped the shrimp from their bags into a larger reed basket that he pulled from under the desk. He moistened them quickly with a hand sprayer before putting the lid back on. "You'll need a receipt," he said, and wrote it out on onionskin paper. He read it back to them. "That's sixty shrimp total. Well done! As soon as you get back out there, we can really lick this problem."

Barthes tickled the moustache of the shrimp in front of him. "Individually they're quite winsome. Would you like to keep one?" After a moment of discussion, they decided that they would. Barthes lifted one out, held it in the air, and sprayed it down again with water. The shrimp seemed to enjoy it, flipping its head back and forth—cheerfully, it seemed, though it was really impossible to say what its mood was, as its expression did not change at all.

"You can buy a sprayer anywhere," he told them. "You might consider it."

"They're charming," said Connie. "I am going to dress it in a bonnet and roll it around in a carriage. I've always wanted a little sister."

"I don't think it will like that very much," said Vera as they left the office.

"Are you sure of that? For all you know it will like the attention."

"Maybe," said Vera, and explored in her mind the image of the shrimp wearing her own dolls' clothes.

Then the jingle in their pockets moved them, as jingles in pockets will, down the road.

## XIII

Now both girls were flush with coins. Vera carried a souvenir change purse from Earth, decorated with a photo of the onion domes in Red Square. Connie's change purse was also from Earth, and it showed a picture of the Capitol Building in Washington, DC. They compared them and laughed.

"Very nice, very nice," they both said, and each kissed her respective landmark.

Vera examined the currency, the first of her own that she had received on the planet. There were no portraits of Sobekis on these coins, but rather, elegant depictions of flora and fauna that appeared, like Roman coins, to have been hand-stamped when the metal was hot. "This must be simple to counterfeit," said Vera, turning a coin over in her hand.

"It's the weight of the metal, not the shape," said Connie.

They each considered the problem of counterfeiting for a moment or two, as had so many Sobeki children and adults before them. It was true you might simply coin your own if you could lay your hands on the material, which meant that there were many strange coins in circulation, and that it was impossible for Sobeki coin collectors to be completists. Of course, it was not easy to lay hands on the metal, for you had to have the same amount of money to buy it.

"The candy store is near here," said Connie. "Let's go. It's considered good luck to spend a little of your earnings as soon as you've gotten them."

Vera agreed eagerly.

The candy shop was crowded with children when Vera and Connie entered. Though it was a nice space, and well-maintained, it had particularly sandy floors. The children came in and out all day and flung the doors open—ignoring the sign that told them not to—and the draft they made drew the sand in. There were always small drifts in the corners.

"They take their candy very seriously here, and even have fancy training colleges. People from all over the world—and sometimes from other planets—come here to attend them." Connie had assumed her position of lecture in front of the store, with her arms behind her back like a tour guide. "Some of the candy on Sobek is just the same as we have on Earth, you know. There is even chocolate here."

Vera was surprised to hear that. "Does it grow in beans, like on Earth?"

Connie did not know, but she supposed it had to be something like that. "It must, because it tastes just the same. They sell it in little vacuum-packed pouches, but still the chocolate doesn't do well in the sun. I always buy it on the way back home unless I plan to eat it right away. Otherwise it can get unpleasant in your pocket; the pouches aren't perfect, and they usually spring a leak.

"They have something like sugar here, too, and make all kinds of lollypops and hard candies," Connie said, pointing to the platters and buckets around them on the tables. Before them was an enormous array of all sorts of sugar constructions spun into thread, grown into honeycombs and blocks of crystal, and tatted into very fragile lacework. There were lollypops shaped like flowers in the full spectrum of color, and some even that glinted as if they had been cut from silvery slabs of mica. There was something like rock candy, but with the sugar growing outward in tendrils from the stick. "They do the rock candy experiment in science class here just like on Earth, but the results are different." Connie did not know the reason why. "I only did the experiment on Earth. I missed it when they did it here."

Connie picked up one of the lollypops. "These are very nice. It is shaped like a particular flower that grows in the gardens here. Everybody is very fond of it." She offered the lollypop to Vera to smell. "They are scented with its nectar as well, so that if you carry them around outside, you must be very careful about bees. They land in the middle to feed, and do not even know the difference."

Vera looked over the store with a feeling she couldn't pinpoint. Before her were all the children from the town who had stayed behind for the Broomstick Holiday; it was not as empty of children as it had seemed to her at first. They were laughing and whistling and hopping around, swatting each other cheerfully, holding intense conferences about the allocation of their funds, making too much noise, and being reprimanded repeatedly by the owner, who shook her finger at them when things got too loud. The children were voluble but not bad, and they lowered their voices politely when reminded, save for one child who had to be removed bodily by an irate mother.

Vera remembered clearly the candy store on the corner near her old school, and the way the children rushed in at the end of the day, and were a nuisance, and paid out fists full of change to cram their mouths full.

"It's like this every day at certain hours," said Connie, but Vera knew as much from Earth.

The owner noticed Vera and Connie and called them over,

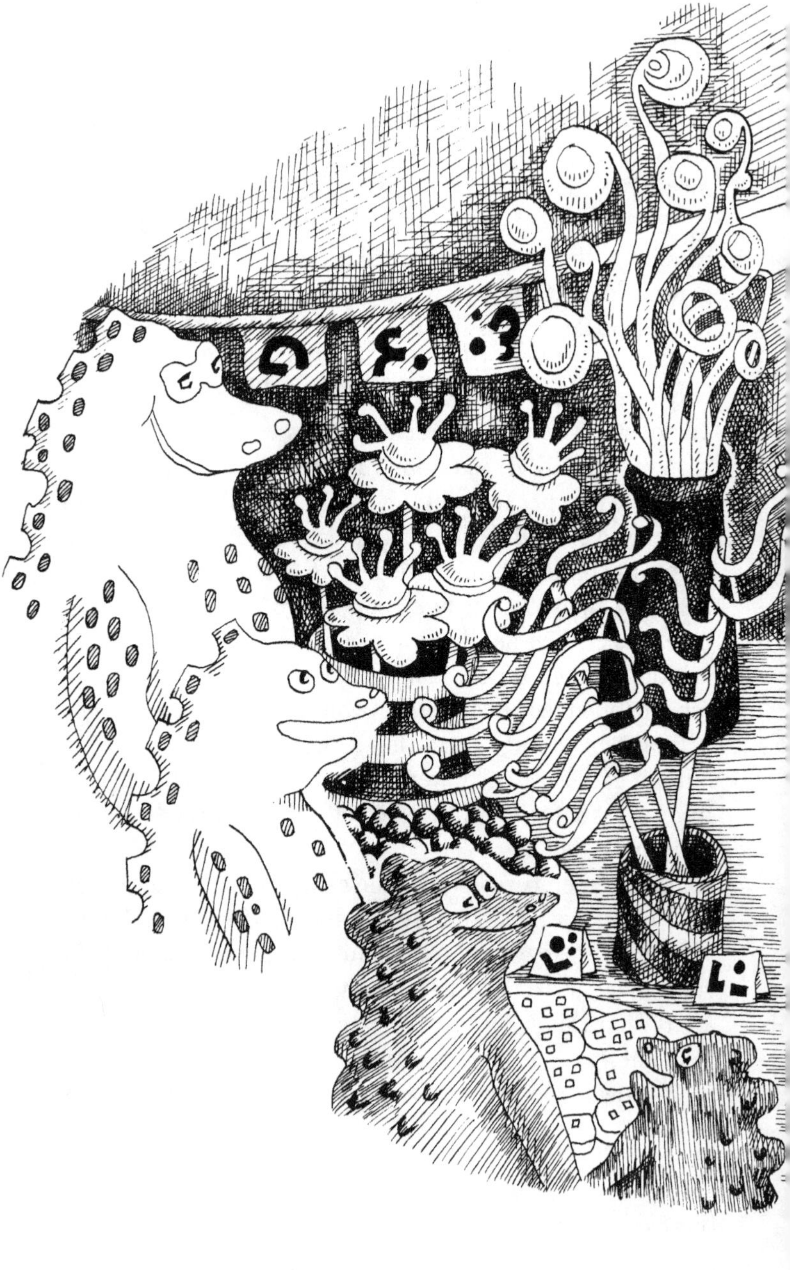

# ORPHAN

HOLD
DO NOT SHIP

H1 – 000000000261

ISBN 9781939333049

| | |
|---|---|
| CLIENT | Alternate Sourcing |
| STATION | TPP Receiving Station 03 |
| HELD | 2026 – 10 – 08 08:51 |

SHELF

If its order arrives, scan this label at a receiving station.

bringing out a series of small cups filled with candy to sample. "You will have the candy before you have the fresh fruit it is made from," Connie translated for the owner. "That's a shame." But the owner chuckled, and clearly did not think that it was such a bad thing, though she pretended to.

Vera took a small sliver of pink hard candy from the tray. It had the fine taste of a blooming flower, though none she had smelled before. Next there was a blue candy that tasted quite metallic—perhaps it was only her own nose, she didn't know—and a brackish candy that she did not like at all, and that made her eyes leak a little.

"That will grow on you," said the shopkeeper, offering her a glass of water. "You will be back for that tomorrow."

Vera smiled, but only after drinking the whole glass.

Some of the candies were strange and some delightful, but as she tasted them Vera felt a uniform happiness fill her, a fondness for the odd sweets that she had never tasted before and for the owner who was so familiar to her, down to her striped apron and the pencil she chewed as she tabulated receipts.

Vera had come very far to be here in this dim and sandy store, surrounded by the exuberant songs of lizard children and the chiding songs of their adults, by the faint smell of grass that was that popular lotion the Sobekis liked to use, and the touch of their cool skin as they brushed by her.

Her world, she knew, was only a faintly glowing thought to them, if it was anything at all. But her friends from Earth could not have imagined Sobek either, and if they thought of it now, it was only because she had come here. She herself had never given it a passing thought before, and suddenly here she was, standing on Sobek with a strange ball of sweet cobwebs in her mouth—she could think of no other way to describe the sensation—and a new friend, Connie, who was standing in front of her, pointing to a poster on the wall.

The world around her was full of new things, but it did not seem as hard as it had seemed before to find a place among them. You might find a place for yourself just by leaving your house and looking around. There was a lot to see.

Then it was her job to write back home and share it with those people who might never be lucky enough even to take a rocket ship off of the Earth! There were many such people in her neighborhood. Old people, certainly, but even children like her, who might never have the opportunity, for one reason or another, to leave their planet. Or really, they would never even want to go.

Vera knew she was not a person like that, for as much as she loved Moscow—its tufty old swans, and the natatorium in which she practiced her dead-man's float—she wanted to know the rest of it, too. For the galaxy is very large, with many places to practice one's floats, and many winged creatures who might like you to feed them peanuts, or something like them.

And there were many things, too, that Vera could not yet imagine, but which would not be at all like her own swimming pool and swans. Many people to meet and share meals with, many animals to learn about, both wild and domesticated; there would be spores and flowers and bacteria and wastelands empty except for rocks and sand. Vera, from here in this cramped candy store, might go anywhere she chose and make it home, as her parents always had.

The cobwebs dissolved on her tongue, and she smiled at the owner.

"Yes," said the owner. "Those are very popular."

Vera chose the candy she wanted, with Connie's help figuring out the prices. When both of them had their paper bags full to go, Connie stopped her and said, "We must have a few of these as well." She added to their orders several handfuls of what she said was bubblegum. They thanked the owner and said goodbye, and went outside to sit in the shade of a Chu-it tree.

"You do not buy it because it tastes good, exactly," said Connie, holding up the bubble gum. "It always tastes the same. One flavor." She and Vera popped the gum into their mouths.

"Like anise," said Vera, and Connie nodded.

"So you chew it up like normal, and when you blow your bubble, just when it's at its largest—hold on, I can't talk and do it." Connie stopped talking and blew the bubble. Then she paused, held up her finger, and blew a tiny breath more. The bubble turned very hard, almost the way that blown glass goes from a molten state to a hard one as it cools.

"Put your hand out to catch it," said Connie, doing just that. "Otherwise, it will fall right in the sand. The little kids always drop theirs. It takes some practice not to, as it's quite slippery."

The Sobeki children usually spat in their hands to clean the candies off before popping them back in their mouths, but that always made their mothers and fathers very angry, so they would do it behind their backs. Of course, if there was a water fountain they could use that to clean off the sand, but some of the worst children liked to watch their parents puff up and get angry, especially if the parents were the types who worried about germs. Parents are the same everywhere.

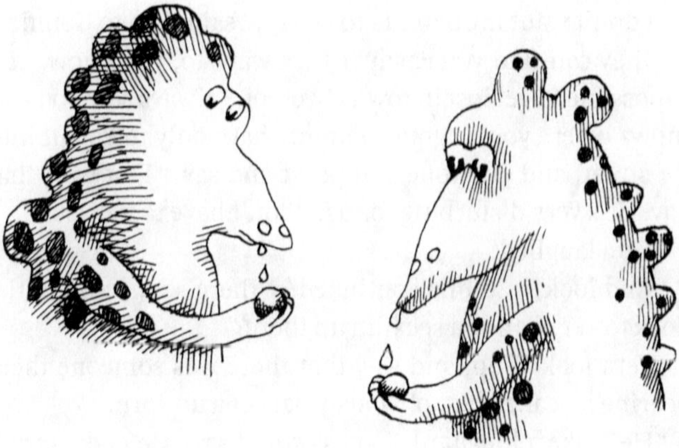

*Despite all counsel from their parents, and all sense of propriety, too, Sobeki children clean off their gumballs with spit.*

Vera tried it and caught her bubble immediately. "What do you do with it now?"

"You eat it," said Connie, who was licking the candy gingerly, for it was a real jawbreaker, and could not be crammed into one's cheek. Eventually, she cracked it and chewed up the shards. Vera followed suit.

They ate their way through quite a bit of their bags, until they were very thirsty from all the sugar. Then they ate a little more. Only after that did they go to find a fountain.

From atop a tall, thin building, a clock chimed. What it chimed Vera didn't know, for it wasn't tolling the hour, but playing a series of somewhat discordant melodies. Perhaps it was not even a clock chiming, but the echoing sound reminded Vera of one, and the sun was going down. Vera was sure she should be heading home.

“I don’t want my parents to worry,” said Vera to Connie.

“They can find you easily if they want to, you know. It’s impossible to get lost in town. Everyone always sees you and knows where you’ve gone. Parents have only to go out into the street, and everyone will point and say, ‘That way, that way!’ It’s very disturbing for us, I don’t have to tell you.”

Vera laughed.

“And look,” Connie continued. “There’s a person in the clock tower. Can you see him up there?”

Vera looked up, and saw that there was someone there wearing a peaked hat, obviously part of a uniform.

“He’s like a lifeguard, I guess you’d say. He takes care if he sees anything amiss, but only for children, of course. It’s in his contract that he can’t testify as to the behavior of the adults.”

Vera laughed again. “What if someone’s mugged?”

“No one will be mugged,” said Connie. “Not seriously.”

“What can he do from way up there?” Vera asked. “He’s miles too far away if anything were to happen.”

“There’s a system,” said Connie vaguely. “I can’t remember what exactly. I’ve heard it’s extremely efficient, though. Little bells ring, and the Custodian of the Square hears them and responds.”

“Well, that’s not how we do it on Earth, I’m sure you remember,” said Vera. Tinkling bells did not seem to her a good response in the face of an emergency, though why not she wasn’t sure. Perhaps it was a fine response, if they could be heard. Connie blew a gentle raspberry, and Vera laughed.

Before they left the fountain, Vera and Connie wet down their shrimp under the spigot. Then they walked back in the direction of their houses. As the sun set, a cool breeze rose from the desert, and by the time the girls were at Vera's street, Vera found herself quite comfortable. She thought she might even need a sweater soon.

They said goodbye at Vera's gate. "See you tomorrow if you'd like," said Connie.

Vera gave her a thumbs up and a smile.

"I'll pick you up at nine, good neighbor!" Connie walked on to her own house, which was only a few blocks away.

Vera waved goodbye and unlatched the gate. She didn't even notice how strange was the building to which she returned or the odd plants growing around it. Perhaps she even thought, "Oh, it's good to be home," as she stepped inside the door of the stone house and into the cool living room. She took off her shoes and placed them on the floor, which was decorated with a mosaic of Quanx shells. It was a beautiful but common shell on Sobek, found empty all over the landscape, as the Quanx crawls out of its shell in the heat of each day and, an adventurer by disposition, generally prefers to find itself somewhere new to live by nightfall.

# XIV

THE shrimp peered out of Vera's bag, sniffed at the air, and seemed quite content with it. Its feelers rippled from side to side. Her parents, who had not spent enough time out of the house, were pleased to have the outside brought to them, and did not mind that she had returned with one from the invasive species.

"It seems somewhat less menacing than the mayor made it out," said her father, taking the shrimp from her by its segmented middle and examining it.

"But they're everywhere in the fountain," Vera said. "It's not relaxing."

"Well, one-on-one they seem perfectly nice," said her mother, taking it from her father and eyeing it. "Were you planning on bringing it back?"

"No. I thought I might keep it for a pet."

"Ah!" said her father enthusiastically. "Better to make a friend than to eat one. Though Vera, we don't know how it will take to captivity. For some animals the strain is immeasurable."

"Bozhe moi!" said her mother. "Your first pet on Sobek!" She went for the camera and posed Vera several ways with the shrimp by her head. Then her mother went into the yard to retrieve a big metal pan that she thought might be good for a terrarium.

"I don't think it's right to keep it in the house. Then, if it absolutely doesn't want to be contained, it can walk away." Vera's mother addressed the last comment kindly to Vera's

*Clearly, the shrimp is considering when to hop over the edge and saunter back to the center of town.*

father, who had once become overly enmeshed in the emotional needs of the family's pet hamster and suffered greatly because of it.

Her father smiled. "Perhaps it will only make its way back to the fountain again."

Together, Vera and her mother found some nice rocks to put inside the pan, and poured several jugs of water into it. Vera took the shrimp and placed it on a rock. It tripped into the water, and stayed under there motionless for a long while before returning to the surface.

"Very good," said her father. "A fine job with the shrimp. It seems extremely comfortable."

Her parents had been sitting at the dining table when she got home. For the first time, Vera noticed that the scene there looked much the same as it would have on Earth. There were only slight differences. They had their papers arrayed, with the large pencil sharpener in the middle of the table. There was a plate of half-eaten cookies—for when they were working they would bite into one and forget all about it—except she knew from sight that the cookies were of a strange flavor, and tasted a bit like a hedgerow. There were glasses of water and cups of coffee, and there was her father's pipe, unlit and listing to the side in the little saucer with the painted kitten that he always used for that purpose.

"How was Connie?" her mother asked.

"She reminds me almost exactly of Isabella Demetrovna at school," said Vera, sitting down with them. "You know, the one who talks a little too much but is really well-liked anyway. She even has the same eyes."

"I remember her," said Vera's mother. "She slept over once and wouldn't eat the eggs we made for breakfast."

"Yes, that's Connie. She has her likes and dislikes."

"Opinionated," said her father, lighting his pipe.

"She doesn't drink milk or eat anything from animals."

"Is that so?" asked her father, well-pleased by that.

"Yes, and she's a little haughty about our ears and things."

"Well, we do look very strange to them."

Her parents pushed aside their papers, and Vera laid out the Sobeki candy on the table to show them. She told them in detail about her day, all the people she had met, some who were quite rude and some who were delightful. Her parents were both very pleased to hear her descriptions.

"You will have to take us around when we have a day off," said Vera's father.

"Yes, you must teach us the local manners and ways," said

her mother. "We don't have enough time for on-the-ground research. Why don't you take some notes for us?"

"Yes, I will," said Vera. "They are very different from us." She thought about all the ways they were different, but they did many things just exactly the same, too. And then there was Connie, who was as much an Earth girl as Vera herself.

Each parent tried a piece of bubble gum, but neither one of them could hold on to it once it had hardened. Vera retrieved her mother's bubble from the floor, wiped the sand off on her shirt, and popped it into a glass of water. It floated on the surface where it fizzed appealingly, and turned the water a lovely shade of teal. Then Vera handed it back to her mother, who gamely took a sip.

"It's quite fragrant," said her mother.

Vera's father would not even pick his up. "That's ridiculous!" he said to the suggestion that he should, and kicked it under a dresser that stood in the corner, to which spot several antlered bugs could soon be seen marching. Vera and her mother laughed and offered him another. When his bubble set the second time, Vera's mother put her hand out to catch it, and then she dropped it into his water glass. "It's all right, I suppose. Novelty candy is never very tasty," he said, and finished his drink. "But you shouldn't have too many, Vera. The Devil knows what's in it!"

That night, the ambassador was set to deliver the speech over which Vera's parents had been laboring. It would be aired after the dinner hour, and they planned to watch it at a café down the street where the owner kept a television. After they finished eating—noodles with a sauce that smelled particularly of haw—they got their sweaters and went out to pick up Alfonse at his house.

"Excellent stars!" he said upon opening the door. "Ideal for strolling."

The stars were clear, even in town, and Alfonse stopped several times on their way to point out important Sobeki constellations like the Glass of Juice and the Cavorting Bathers. He promised to lend Vera's parents a book of Sobeki constellations on the return home.

"You must learn them soon," he cautioned. "Otherwise, you won't be able to make evening small talk."

There were only a few Sobekis in the café. They were intent on a Sobeki opera, and grumbled when Vera's parents asked to change the channel. "This is that fellow's debut, you know. First time in the role, that means," one Sobeki told them. "Besides, I don't suppose the ambassador has anything new to say." But after Vera's parents explained that they had written the speech, everyone agreed to put it on.

The sour ambassador was just beginning his remarks. He spoke crossly about an upcoming exchange program. There was to be a tour of hospitality from a group of Earth people, and a Sobeki group would soon be visiting Earth as well. "This tour will ignite the match of caring between our civilizations," he said, and Alfonse smiled, as it was a line he had added when walking through the room.

"I'm still not entirely sure what is meant by 'igniting the match of caring,'" said Vera's father to her mother under his breath. "Why does the caring have to be on fire?"

"I'm not certain," said Vera's mother, "though it is the quickest way to spread it."

After speaking for a reasonable length of time—Vera's parents were relieved that the ambassador did not begin to speak extemporaneously in his garbled Sobeki, as he some-

*The Moonswept Café down the street from the Mironovs lays claim to the distinction that it was the first to ferment the sap of the Indulus tree. Though this is widely known—the drink created from the liquor is even called a Moonswept—it does not stop rival cafés from claiming a role in the drink's development, going so far as to hang signs to that effect in their front windows.*

times did—the ambassador opened the floor to questions.

"He seems somewhat less horrible than the last time I heard him speak," one of the opera lovers said to Vera's parents as she rose to change the channel. "You should congratulate yourselves for discharging an extremely difficult task."

Vera's parents smiled. "He did seem quite a bit more likeable," said Vera's father. "Less antagonistic, even."

"I'm sure it helped that we took out the bit about the bad manners of Sobeki children," said her mother.

"Yes, he has harped on that in every speech up until now," Alfonse agreed. "Our children aren't worse than yours, are they?" he asked with some concern.

"Of course not," said Vera's father. "Our Earth children are unpardonable."

They were all cheerful on the way home, the three adults because of the relatively successful speech, and Vera because she had been offered several bubbly drinks filled with fruit, which seemed to have had some mild but lasting effect on her. "Was I meant to drink that?" she asked her mother.

"That was the children's version," her mother replied.

They dropped Alfonse off at his door, and he asked them to wait for a moment while he went in to find the book of constellations. He had not forgotten, and was quite insistent about it. "Keep it as long as you want," he said on returning, "but *do* make sure you read it—and thoroughly!"

Then Vera and her parents made their way home.

"Shall we sit outside for while?" Vera's mother asked, and they dragged their living room chairs out into the garden. "I gather this is what they like to do in the evening. They make a point of watching the moon rise. 'Just like a new ballad dissolves the lumpish pain in your heart, fresh air dissolves

*These tenacious bugs will take the entire night, if they must, to roll the gumball back to their hole.*

the lump of steak in your stomach,'" Vera's mother said in Sobeki. "A popular expression," she added, and smiled.

"Some of the neighbors like to take an evening dip in the fountain before putting the children to bed," said Vera's father, "but that might take us past the limit of our intrepid spirit for today."

They all agreed with that. It had been a long day.

After arranging themselves comfortably in the garden, Vera and her parents watched as those antlered bugs came by rolling their prize—the hard candy now coated in sand—out the front door. They got it down the steps by shoving it off the top, standing aside while it bounced down, and then retrieving it at the bottom. Then the bugs rolled it away under a rock at the end of the path.

"Hmm," said her father, "those are some peculiar bugs. What will they do with that sand-covered sucking candy?" He puffed thoughtfully on his evening pipe.

"Look, Vera," he said. "I will show you just where our sun should be. You can't see it tonight because it is very faint and the moon is very bright, but just about there is where it is." He pointed with the stem of his pipe to the ridge of the mountains, and made a large circle that seemed to hang visibly in the air. "Somewhere in there," he said.

And "somewhere in there," a little more than a month after this scene took place, a letter from Vera was pinned up on the corkboard by the front door of the Strugatsky School in Moscow. The corkboard had been set aside for news of Vera and her adventures, and had waited patiently. There was a large portrait of her in the middle wearing her medal, and the first letter she sent was now pinned up by Ms Lapidus in pride of place at the top, leaving room for more to come. (This was optimistic, of course, since children can be quite unreliable correspondents.) It was a recounting somewhat similar to what you have just read, though some things were left out and some magnified beyond recognition. Vera had also taken some time with her own illustrations.

Two weeks later, a packet began its journey back to Vera full of letters and small gifts from her friends, classmates and teachers on Earth. What news was in it, we will have to wait until later to find out. It sits at present in the hold of the *Lorraine Wong*, nestled close to a tub of apple butter and a shipment of hand-knit toy humans in regional dress.

Now over the desert, the moon climbed the sky and illuminated that oceanic whiteness. Except for the wind that skimmed the top of the sand, it was very still there. Next to Vera and her parents, the shrimp in its habitat made an uncanny, keening cry that was answered by shrimp all over town. Vera could now name one sound from the cacophony she heard each night, and see the face of the creature who made it, puffed out in a homely manner as it called.

"It's a lonesome sound," said Vera, who was not lonesome at all herself.

"Yet it could jump out of there if it chose to," said her mother. "It doesn't seem particularly wedded to the water, and the walls are not very high."

"Perhaps it is only singing," added Vera's father. "The moon might have stirred it."

A long way off, from out of the desert, Vera could hear the hoots and yowls of other animals. She did not know their names. She did not even know what species they were. Were they birds? Were they lions? They might be anything. The snake with the false face in its markings, the Wild Cutlers that prowled the peripheries hungrily. Still, as she sat in the walled garden with her mother and father, facing out into that unknown view, she felt more curious than afraid.

www.ingramcontent.com/pod-product-compliance
Lightning Source LLC
Chambersburg PA
CBHW061546250926
52052CB00010B/3091
* 9 7 8 1 9 3 9 3 3 3 0 4 9 *